MELONHEAD
AND THE
UNDERCOVER OPERATION

ALSO BY KATY KELLY

MELONHEAD

AND THE
UNDERCOVER OPERATION

BY KATY KELLY
ILLUSTRATED BY GILLIAN JOHNSON

A YEARLING BOOK

A NOTE FROM THE AUTHOR:

The FBI is not currently offering tours. The FBI does train agents in a fake town called Hogan's Alley in Quantico, Virginia.

The Junior Special Agent program is real.

Text copyright © 2011 by Katy Kelly
Cover art and interior illustrations copyright © 2011 by Gillian Johnson

All rights reserved. Published in the United States by Yearling, an imprint of Random House Children's Books, a division of Random House, Inc., New York. Originally published in hardcover in the United States by Delacorte Press, an imprint of Random House Children's Books, New York, in 2011.

Yearling and the jumping horse design are registered trademarks of Random House, Inc.

Visit us on the Web! randomhouse.com/kids

Educators and librarians, for a variety of teaching tools, visit us at randomhouse.com/teachers

The Library of Congress has cataloged the hardcover edition of this work as follows:
Kelly, Katy.
Melonhead and the undercover operation / by Katy Kelly ; illustrated by Gillian Johnson. — Hardcover trade ed.
p. cm.
Summary: Ten-year-old Adam (Melonhead) Melon and his fellow Junior Special Agent, Sam, investigate a fellow resident of Washington D.C.'s Capitol Hill neighborhood, believing that she is one of the FBI's Ten Most Wanted.
ISBN 978-0-385-73659-6 (hardcover) — ISBN 978-0-385-90618-0 (glb) —
ISBN 978-0-375-98292-7 (ebook) [1. Spies—Fiction. 2. Behavior—Fiction. 3. Family life—Washington (D.C.)—Fiction. 4. Washington (D.C.)—Fiction. 5. Humorous stories.]
I. Johnson, Gillian, ill. II. Title.
PZ7.K29637Mgu 2011
[Fic]—dc22
2010039057

ISBN 978-0-375-84528-4 (pbk.)

Printed in the United States of America

10 9 8 7 6 5 4 3

First Yearling Edition 2012

Random House Children's Books supports the First Amendment and celebrates the right to read.

For my sister, Meg Kelly Rizzoli,
who is thoughtful, generous, charming, and a truly original thinker.
Plus, she's hilarious.

1
THE G FOR L

I slid down the banister, raced through the hall and around the dining room table, and hit the swinging kitchen door with both arms out. I go for maximum bounce-back.

"Whoops, sorry, Dad! I didn't know you were there," I said.

My mom was bent over with her head in the fridge. So all I could see was her bottom half. All she could see of me was nothing.

"Go back upstairs and brush your teeth," she said.

"I'm on vacation," I said.

"Personal grooming does not get summers off," she said.

She is psychic about hygiene.

"Once I eat breakfast they'll be dirty all over again. The next thing you know, it's lunch."

"And the next thing you know, you'll have so many cavities your teeth will look like Swiss cheese," she said. "Go brush."

"Sam and I are going to the FBI," I explained.

My mom popped up. She forgot the freezer door was open. That's hard on a head. Believe me. I know.

"Adam," she said. "Come here."

She's practically the only one who calls me that. It beats her other name for me, which is Darling Boy. I'm trying to get her to stop saying DB in front of people. It's not going well. Getting her to call me by my usual name of Melonhead is hopeless.

She used the refrigerator sponge to wipe the dried-up crud off my navy blue Federal Bureau of Investigation T-shirt. It came from a street vendor.

"Don't wash my Junior Special Agent badge," I said.

My badge came from the FBI. It is one hundred percent real.

"Teeth," she said.

"How about I brush twice tonight?" I asked her.

My dad was at the table, doodling with one hand and rubbing his head with the other. "Get going, Sport."

"Dad, you're the one who said I should be a Man of My Word. My word to Sam was 'See you at eight-thirty a.m.'"

He smiled.

"Mom," I said. "It's rude to keep my best friend waiting. And you're the anti-rudest person in Washington, D.C."

Her eyebrows jumped up. Bouncing eyebrows mean that she is fed up.

"I'm going," I said.

"Brush until you've counted to one hundred in your head," my mom said.

To save time I counted by twos.

When I came back down my dad was burning his fingers getting my bagel, egg, and double ketchup sandwich out of the microwave.

"I'll eat it while I walk to the Alswangs'," I said.

"We need to have a family conversation before I leave for the airport," my dad said.

We have a talk every time he goes to Florida. We used to live there before we moved to Washington, D.C., for my dad's job that keeps sending him on trips to Florida.

He likes to discuss Things That Should Not Happen while he's away. My mom's topic is usually Things That Have Gone Wrong in the Past. Then my dad says I've learned from my mistakes. My mom says she hopes so.

"Sometimes it's impossible to know if a thing is a mistake until I'm in a situation," I explained. "Sometimes I don't know I'm in a situation until somebody tells Mom and she tells me. Sam has the same problem."

"The neighbors say that too," my mom said.

"Pop says Sam and I are proof of great minds thinking alike," I said.

Pop is our good old friend. I mean old like between sixty and seventy and also old like a long time. We met when I moved here, two and a half years ago, which is one quarter of my life.

"Just check the Remind-O-Rama before you do anything," my mom said.

She invented the Remind-O to improve my judgment.

"It doesn't work," I told her.

"Which is why I'm introducing the New and Improved, Easy-to-Master, Fun-to-Follow Melon Family Guidelines for Life," my dad said. "Instead of telling you what not to do." He handed me his doodled-on napkin.

"Read out loud so I can hear," my mom said.

1. *Think About Cause and Effect.*
2. *Plan Ahead.*
3. *Consider Consequences.*
4. *When in Doubt, Ask an Adult.*
5. *If You Do Something Wrong, Make It Right.*
6. *Take Personal Responsibility.*
7. *Honesty Is the Only Policy.*
8. *Remember the Ways of Ladies.*
9. *Think of Others.*

My mom was so excited she swallowed a hunk of peach whole.

"I will create a Guidelines for Life poster for the kitchen," she said.

Making posters about behavior is her hobby.

"Sport?" my dad asked.

"Don't you worry," I said. "These G for Ls are so simple a worm could do them."

He smiled and stirred up my hair with his fingers.

"You can break a Guideline if it's an emergency, right?" I asked.

"An emergency?" he said.

"Like if Sam and I have to rescue a baby," I said.

"It is rare that a baby needs rescuing," he said.

"But *if* a baby is *dangling from a windowsill*, I should reel it in, right, Dad?"

"Right," he said. "All rules are suspended for dangling babies."

"Or if a two-year-old is *crawling on the Southwest Freeway*, I should save it," I said.

"Absolutely," he said.

"Letting a baby crawl on a freeway is what I call careless parenting," my mom said.

"What if somebody is getting pecked in the head by wild pigeons?" I asked. "Do I ask an adult before I chase the birds away? What if it's an adult getting pecked? Can that adult give permission?"

"Sport," my dad said. "Have you ever seen a flock of attack pigeons on Capitol Hill?"

"I've seen bats," I said.

"Attack bats?" he asked.

"They could have been," I said.

"Wild pigeons pecking would be a case of act first, ask later," my dad said. "The same goes for bat attacks."

There was banging on the back-door window.

"Melonhead! You were supposed to come get me," Sam yelled.

"Leave your skateboard on the porch and come in," my mom said.

"Sam, my Junior G-man," my dad said. "I'm off to Pensacola for a few days.

I'm counting on you to help your pal follow the new Melon Family Guidelines for Life while I'm gone."

"Count away," Sam said. "We won't bring anything that's disgusting, muddy, or alive into the house."

"You are reading Mrs. Melon's mind," my dad said.

"Part of my mind," she said. "The other part is thinking about last month's Superior Sound Machine experiment."

"Remember what Dad said," I told her. "The guy who invented omelets had to break lots of eggs."

"I hope you don't have to break any more dryers," she said.

"I don't think we will," Sam told her.

"You have to admit spinning rocks sound like dinosaurs destroying New York," I said.

"To be safe, let's say no using appliances while I'm gone," my dad said.

"Even my electric toothbrush?" I asked.

"You can use that," he said. "But only on teeth."

"Deal," Sam said.

"His teeth," my mom said.

"Mom," I said. "You can relax like an old dog. Everything we are doing today is not troublesome."

"Terrific," my dad said. "I hope your next tour of the FBI is as interesting as the first one."

"It will be," I said. "It's the same tour every time."

"You're loyal visitors," my mom said. "They should promote you from Junior Specials to Honorary Agents."

"That would be like getting fired," I said. "Honoraries don't get to do actual agent stuff, like ride in speeding cars and chase crooks."

My mom sucked in her breath. *They let Junior Agents go on crook-chasing car chases?"* she said. "Because that is one permission slip I will never sign!"

Panic makes her voice squeak.

My dad smiled and squeezed my mom's shoulder. "Junior Agents don't get to go on car chases, Betty."

"That's true," Sam said. "We asked."

I could tell my dad was holding back a laugh.

"Don't tease me for believing," my mom said. "People let kids do dangerous things these days.

Remember when your brother asked Adam if he wanted to go parasailing? What if I hadn't been there to say Not in This Lifetime?"

I would have gotten to parasail, that's what.

My dad's phone buzzed.

"My cab's out front," he said. "Betty, let's have a smooch."

They kissed. Sam says that's embarrassing. I agree.

"I'll miss you," my dad said.

"We'll miss you more," my mom told him.

They say the same mush every time he leaves.

"I call rolling your suitcase down the steps!" I yelled.

"Go fast for maximum wheel bumps," Sam said.

"Of course, Horse," I said.

The next thing that happened was a shock.

"Who knew a suitcase wheel could split in half?" Sam said.

"Don't worry, Dad," I said. "It still rolls. Only now it's like smooth-bump-twist, smooth-bump-twist."

"Great," my dad said. "I'll enjoy bump-twisting my way through the airports."

"You're a fun-loving kind of adult, Mr. Melon," Sam said.

My dad carried his suitcase by the handle.

"You know, it's heavier that way," I said.

"I do know," my dad said.

Then he jumped in the Diamond Taxi. Then he yelled through the window. "Back in a flash."

That's another thing he always says.

2

GOING UNDERGROUND

My mom got two subway tickets off the bulletin board. "These will get you to the FBI and back," she said. "And here's in-case-of-emergency money."

"Thanks," I said.

My mom held my cheeks and looked at me eyeballs to eyeballs. "Do not stand close to the tracks. Pay attention. Get off at the right stop. Mind your manners. Don't get in the way of other riders."

"Yes, ma'am," I said.

She looked at Sam and back at me. "Do not sit when elderly people are standing. Don't push, shout, or bounce around on the train. Do not talk to strangers."

"I know, Mom," I said.

"Daddy insists that you are old enough to ride the Metro alone," she said. "Show me that he's right."

"You say that every time," I said.

She smiled. "No chasing crooks in fast cars!" she said.

Then she laughed to show that was a joke.

"Say goodbye, McFly," Sam said to me.

I waved. "Let's leave, Steve."

If there was a job called rhymer, Sam and I would get it.

The Metro is a deal. Once you put your ticket in the slot, you can ride all day for one fare as long as you don't go through the EXIT gates until the end. Last summer, my mom visited her college roommate in Birmingham, Alabama, for three days. I got to stay at the Alswangs'. Sam and I rode the yellow, red, orange, and green lines back and forth for five hours and twenty-six minutes. Pop says he does not know another person who has done that on purpose. If there was one, he would have heard. Believe me. Pop has lived on Capitol

Hill his whole life. He was alive when the Metro got built.

Sam and I reported our subway time to *Guinness World Records*. We haven't heard back yet.

When we got to Union Station, Sam screamed, "Onetwothreego!"

That means Escalator Race. ERs are not for chickens or people with shoelaces. Metro escalators are so long, some people get so nervous they have to take the elevators. My mom is one of them.

At the bottom I told Sam, "I would have won except people were blocking my way."

"You'd think adults would know it's rude to get in the way of other riders," he said.

The light-up sign said nine minutes until the next train. Standing around on the platform is dull as mayonnaise. Brick-tile floors are unslidable in sneakers.

"We can fit on that bench if we squeeze in between people," I told Sam.

To be friendly, Sam asked the man sitting next to him, "How are you?"

"Squished," the man said.

"I know what you mean," I said. "These benches are too small."

The yellow-haired lady on the edge next to me said, "I recognize you boys."

"You do?" Sam asked.

"I've seen you bike-riding around Eastern Market."

"We go there a lot," I said. "Mostly because of Baking Divas."

"Best bakery on Capitol Hill," she said. "Best croissants outside Paris."

"We're personal friends with the owners," I said.

"Also one owner's daughter," Sam said. "Her name is Jonique. She goes to our school. Jonique and our friend Lucy Rose got desserts named after them."

"Jonique gets to go behind the counter," I said. "And she doesn't have to pay."

"If I had your pal Jonique's job, I'd be filling my mouth and my pockets," the lady said. "There would be nothing left to sell."

That seemed bad to me, but she was laughing.

"Do you live near the Divas?" Sam asked her.

"A block away," she said. "My house is on Eighth Street."

"I bet we've seen it," I said.

"It has a tower on top, and a red door and an ugly green bay window," she said.

"How ugly?" Sam asked.

"It's only ugly on the outside," she said. "From the inside it's perfect. I can spy on the whole neighborhood. The other day I saw two bike-riding boys crash into my azalea bushes. On purpose, I think."

"They might be some other boys," I said. "It's hard to tell with helmets."

Which my mother makes me wear even if I'm going for a three-feet-long ride.

"And I believe I've been behind you in line at Capital City Savings and Loan," she said.

"Melonhead and I go to that bank two times a day," Sam said.

She smiled. "You must have a lot of money."

"We do," Sam said. "We follow their motto: Make Your Money Work for You!"

"Our money works every time," I said. "Believe me."

She looked like she didn't.

"In the morning Melonhead gets one dollar out of his savings," Sam said.

"Then Sam puts my dollar in his account," I said.

"Then the teller hands me a Dum Dum lollipop. For free," Sam said.

"In the afternoon, we do it in reverse and I get the sucker," I said.

"When I got up this morning I had no idea I was going to meet a couple of whiz kids," she said.

"Thank you," Sam said.

She stuck out her hand for us to shake. "My name is Bethany Lewis," she said.

When the train came I told her, "Ms. Lewis, you may get on first, please."

Sam leapt ahead of her and blocked the sideways seat in front. "This one's for you, Ms. Lewis," he yelled. "You're the priority."

"I'm thirty-eight!" she said. "I'm NOT a senior citizen."

"Anybody can tell that," Sam said.

"I hope so," Ms. Lewis said.

"He meant you're priority because you're having a baby," I said.

"I am *not* having a baby!" she said.

"Are you sure?" I asked. "Your stomach is puffed out."

"I'm quite sure," she said.

"You probably just eat a lot," I said.

"Let's change the subject," she said.

"Okay," Sam said. "Where are you getting off?"

"The Smithsonian," she said. "I'm going to see the Hope Diamond at the natural history museum."

"It's as big as a gorilla eyeball," Sam said.

"But it has a curse on it," I told her.

"I think I could live with a curse for an eyeball-size diamond," she said.

"We're going to the J. Edgar Hoover Building," Sam said.

"Also known as the FBI," I told her.

"Aka the Federal Bureau of Investigation," Sam said.

"I've never been," she said.

"Are you kidding?" I asked.

"We are Junior Special Agents," Sam told her.

"If you don't believe him, look at this." I showed her my badge.

Sam opened the duct tape wallet I made him for Hanukkah and took out a card. "This is my genuine, official Junior Special Agent ID."

"Plus we have certificates at home," I said.

"How did you get to be Junior Special Agents?" Ms. Lewis asked.

"First you have to be Junior Special Agents in Training," Sam said. "It takes weeks before you get to take the oath."

"Tell me about the training," she said.

"Actual adult agents came to our school," Sam said. "They showed us how to take fingerprints and a polygraph, which is the same as a lie detector."

"The Evidence Response Team showed us how one hair reveals if a person is a criminal," I told her.

"If the person left one hair at the crime," Sam said, "which happens more than you'd think."

"One hair?" Ms. Lewis asked.

"If criminals were smart, which they aren't, they'd wear hats when they're robbing," I told her.

"They'd still get caught," Sam said.

"True," I said. "FBI agents are brilliant times in- finity."

"You can come with us," Sam said.

"I'd sooner tour a swamp," Ms. Lewis said.

"That's a hard choice," I said. "I've been in the

Everglades in Florida. It's the king swamp of all swamps. I saw alligators, and a vulture carrying a dead snake. Plus I got over one hundred bug bites. It was one of the top days of my life."

"I don't see how the FBI can compete with vultures and dead things," Ms. Lewis said.

For no reason the man sitting next to her laughed.

"I'll tell you how," Sam said. "The FBI has FATS."

"I am interested in fats," she said. "Especially olive oil."

"FATS stands for FireArms Training System," I said. "That means Weapons."

"Oh, my," she said.

"If you ever meet Melonhead's mother, don't mention the weapons," Sam said. "Her nerves are weak."

"Where are these FATs?" Ms. Lewis asked.

"In Quantico, Virginia, at a Marine base," I said.

"You boys know a lot about crime and punishment," Ms. Lewis said. "Are you planning to be agents when you grow up?"

"After I get done being a professional baseball player," Sam said.

"I'm going to invent gadgets for agents," I said. "I already turned a mustard squirting bottle into a Robber Stopper. I'm thinking about giving it to the lady at the bank."

"How does it work?" she asked.

"Really well," I said.

She threw her head back and laughed. "You're a good boy," she said.

"Thanks," I said. "A lot of people don't notice."

When we got off she said, "So long, whiz kids!"

"She's my kind of grown-up," I said.

3

FUGITIVES FROM JUSTICE

We walked through the FBI's mega-enormous front door and ran to be first in the tour line.

Agent Sabrina Atkin said, "Hello, Junior Special Agents," right off the bat. She always tells tourists we're her colleagues. That means we work together.

A short lady wearing a Penn State T-shirt gave us a thumbs-up.

I enjoy being praised.

Agent Atkin is one hundred percent excellent. She knows the ways of masterminds and forgers. Plus she's an expert on olden-days criminals like Bonnie and Clyde. Sam and I know the tour by heart. We ask questions anyway. That's a help to tourists.

A lady with a plaid dress and twin five-year-old boys was behind us. Sam and I think young kids are too childish for the tour.

"Can anybody be an FBI agent?" a gray-haired lady asked.

"Only the best," Agent Atkin said. "Agents need skills and commitment, courage, intelligence, loyalty, and a desire to serve their country."

A man who looked as old as my dad said, "How do you become a Special Agent?"

I whispered, "I'm not being rude but don't try out, sir. Agents have to climb walls and run up fire escapes and hide in the woods. You don't look like you're up to it. No offense."

Agent Atkin coughed. "If you are chosen to be a Special Agent trainee, you'll move into the FBI Academy in Quantico, Virginia, for twenty weeks," she said. "Eight hundred and fifty hours will be spent learning how to investigate, to defend and protect yourself, to search for evidence, to do daytime and nighttime surveillance, to disguise yourself, to fingerprint and handcuff suspects."

"Plus, you get to have paintball gunfights with criminals," I told the tourists.

"Criminals?" the man's wife said. "That seems unwise."

Agent Atkin laughed. "The FBI hires actors to act like criminals," she said. "They try to escape, resist arrest, and fight their way out."

"Out of what?" a teenager asked.

"Hogan's Alley," I said.

"Hogan's Alley is a training town we built," Agent Atkin said. "It's got a movie theater, a bank, a post office, a hotel, a Laundromat, and a barbershop."

"Don't forget Honest Jim's used-car lot," Sam said. "And the pool hall."

"It has a deli, homes, shops, even mailboxes," Agent Atkin said. "But it's one tough neighborhood. Kidnappings, holdups, and other crimes happen every day."

"It's a fake town," I said.

Agent Atkin exhaled. "Our Junior Special Agent is right," she said. "Everything is fake. There's no money in the bank, no sandwiches in the deli, no people living in the houses. The mailboxes don't open. There are real cars at Honest Jim's but they're not really for sale."

Everybody always wants to know the details about Hogan's Alley.

When the tour was over Sam told the teenager, "You should see the Ten Most Wanteds."

Most tourists only look at the MWs for about thirty seconds. Sam and I study them. MWs are so terrible they don't call them crooks. They call them Fugitives from Justice. When we were in third grade, Sam and I thought *fugitive* was a good thing. But our friend Lucy Rose, who is a word maniac, told us it means they are *on the lam*, which is the same as *hiding from the law*.

Sam socked my arm. "Look out, *crook out!*

Johnny Douglas, alias Doug Johns, Jr., alias Snake, is off the wall!"

Right across the fugitive's face, in red capital letters, it said: APPREHENDED!

"Captured!" I said. "Slammed in the slammer!"

"Nabbed in Chattanooga, Tennessee," Sam said. "Right in front of the Pancakery."

"Those customers must have been thinking, *This is the luckiest day of our lives*," I said. "Just sitting there eating, they look out the window and BAM! A hundred FBI agents leap out of hiding places. The Snake didn't have a sliver of a chance."

"Getting to see an MW captured is my number one wish," Sam said.

"It's pretty much everybody's number one wish, Sam," I said.

"The Snake should have known he'd be caught," Sam said. "An Abraham Lincoln beard is a giveaway of a disguise."

I pointed at the wall. "Whoa, Joe! Look at the replacement criminal."

The second they catch a Most Wanted, the eleventh-worst crook turns into the tenth Most

Wanted. Otherwise, it would be the Nine Most Wanted. After a while they'd run out.

"Wow!" I said. "A lady FFJ! They're rare."

SUSAN BANNON

10th MOST WANTED

BY FBI

REAL NAME : SUSAN BANNON
AKA SUSiE LoUiE
Banyane,
Lou Banny,
Sue Lew,
Lulu Rich,
Lulu du Lanne

NICKNAME : THE CHAMELEON

Date of Birth —	Height —
Marks of Distinguish —	Weight — 135-150s
eyes —	Build, Female new.
Subject $100000	Occupation
	Scars, moles

$ 1,000,000 REWARD

"What a load of aliases!" Sam said. "'Real name: Susan Bannon, aka Susie Louise Banyonne, Lou Banny, Sue Lew, Lulu Rich, Lulu du Lannue. Nickname: The Chameleon.'"

"Criminals go for reptile names," I said.

I leaned over for a close-up view and practically flipped over the railing. "Look!" I said.

"I am," Sam said.

"Do you see her nose?" I asked.

"Of course," Sam said.

"Think of her with different hair. And a skinny neck. And darker eyebrows."

"Why?"

"Don't you get it?" I said. "It's Ms. Lewis!"

"No way," Sam said.

"Picture her in your mind," I said.

"I guess that could be her nose," he said.

"Of course it's her nose."

"Ms. Lewis doesn't have black hair," Sam said.

"She's wearing a wig," I said.

"That's a wig?"

"It has to be," I said. "She had light yellow hair on the Metro."

"Do Ms. Lewis's canine teeth stick out?" he asked.

"Sam, she's called the Chameleon because she changes her looks like a camouflaging reptile. False teeth are nothing to her."

I just figured out her nickname. Before, I thought she was a lizard lover.

"Does Ms. Lewis have a blob for a chin?" Sam asked.

"Oh, she has boxes of chin putty," I said. "Believe me."

"Chin putty?"

"That might not be the exact name of it, but it's what actors use when they need a big chin."

"Like the *Wizard of Oz* witch," Sam said.

I stuck my hands into the side pockets of my cargo shorts and sifted through the Froot Loops and Lucky Charms. I found the two-inch pencil I got for playing miniature golf. It was in my thigh pocket covered with Cheerio dust.

"Stay here," I said. "I'm going for paper."

I ran eight hundred mph. That means miles per hour.

"Write 'The Case of the Missing Chameleon' on the first sheet," I said.

Sam started and stopped. "Toilet paper tears when you write on it," he said.

"Don't press so hard," I told him.

Date of Birth: *Unknown.* **Estimated age:** *Between 35 and 45.*

"Thirty-eight is right between!" Sam said.

Master of Disguise. Hair: *Variable. Has been blond, brown, black, gray, and red. Bannon often wears wigs.*

I punched Sam's arm. "I told you so."

Eyes: *Blue but uses colored contact lenses to make them appear brown, green, and violet.*

"All at once?" Sam asked.
"Probably not," I said.

Subject often wears glasses.

"Ms. Lewis had sunglasses!" I said.

Height: *Approximately 5'5".*
Weight: *Between 135 and 150 pounds.*
Gender: *Female.*
Build: *Medium.*

"She was completely medium," Sam said.

Occupation: *Once worked as a bank teller.*

"The bank!" Sam said. "She admitted she goes to the bank."
"We were duped!" I said.
"And tricked," Sam said.

Nationality: *American.*
Language: *English and French.*

"Remember she knew about *croissants in Paris?*" Sam asked.

Scars and Marks: *Mole on the back of her neck.*

"My Aunt Traci had a family of moles in her yard," I said. "I can identify a mole tattoo in a flash."

"Maybe it's the brown dot kind of mole," Sam said.

"Sam," I said. "If agents were close enough to see the dot kind of mole, they would have sprung the handcuffs on her in a split millisecond."

"You're right, Dwight," Sam said.

Frequents expensive resorts, hotels, restaurants, and vacation spots.

"Washington, D.C., is a vacation spot," I said.

"My Mimi says everything here is expensive," Sam said.

"The proof is piling up," I said.

The Chameleon has family ties in Texas, Wyoming, Hawaii, and Montana, and along the East Coast.

"Washington, D.C., is on the East Coast," I said.

Victims say Bannon appears sympathetic, loyal, honest, intelligent, friendly, and charming.

"To me Ms. Lewis is charming," Sam said.
"Ditto to me," I said.

Modus Operandi: *Skilled at conversation, Bannon befriends wealthy people.*

"She got us to admit we're rich," I said.

Gains victims' trust.

"We trusted," Sam said.

Learns their schedules; gets access to homes, security codes, and valuables.
A cat burglar known to Interpol, Bannon is brazen and fearless and takes risks.
While at a crowded Hollywood party, Bannon slipped into a bedroom closet, cracked the safe, and removed a ruby necklace that once belonged to the Queen

of Siam. Hid the priceless jewels in a secret pocket sewn into the lining of her dress. Returned to the party. Danced with the host before leaving.

Works with an unidentified male.

To date, Bannon has stolen over $100 million in cash, bonds, coins, rare stamps, and jewels.

"The Hope Diamond!" we both said at once.

REWARD: *The FBI is offering a reward of up to $1 million for information leading directly to the arrest of Susan Bannon.*

I shook Sam's shoulders. "Hot diggity dog on a log! We're going to be rich."

"And famous," he said.

CONSIDERED DANGEROUS. *IF YOU HAVE ANY INFORMATION CONCERNING THIS PERSON, PLEASE CONTACT YOUR LOCAL FBI OFFICE OR THE NEAREST U.S. EMBASSY OR CONSULATE.*

"I vote for the FBI," I said. "Because you can only find an American embassy if you're not in America."

"And we don't know what a consulate is," Sam said.

We ran. The marble hall was over-shined. So Sam hit a wall when he turned.

When we could see the guard desk, we waved our arms. "Red Alert! Call for backup!" I said.

"The Chameleon is escaping on the Red Line," Sam yelled.

I collided with the guard's desk.

"The Chameleon?" the guard said. "On the subway?"

"Trust us," I said. "We're Junior Special Agents. She's after the Hope Diamond!"

"Very interesting," the guard said.

"If we'd known it was her when we were with her, we would have made a citizens' arrest," I told him.

"No, you wouldn't," the guard said.

"We don't mind," I said.

"The FBI minds," he said.

"Why?" I asked.

"Sit on those blue visitor chairs," he said, "while I make a call."

That took forever and felt like longer because the scratchy chair cloth was stabbing the backs of my knees.

"I spot a red head," Sam said.

"Agent Atkin!" I said. "Getting off the elevator."

We waved. "Over here," Sam said as loud as he could without yelling.

"Hello again," Agent Atkin said. "Officer Yang says you have information about one of our Most Wanteds."

Sam told the first part. I told the parts he forgot. We tried to keep it in order. You could tell our report was shocking Agent Atkin.

"This city has thousands of middle-aged blond women," she said.

"My mom is one of them," I said. "But hair is only a sliver of the evidence."

"The Chameleon's face is round, exactly like in the picture," Sam said. "Ditto for her nose."

"Her nose is round?" Agent Atkin asked.

"More like a kumquat with nostrils," I said.

"Plus she is medium size," Sam said. "And she personally told us she's thirty-eight years old."

"She has freckles," I said.

"She does?" Sam asked.

"What was she wearing?" Agent Atkin asked.

She was excited. I could tell by her mega-smile.

"A dress," Sam said.

"Or it could be those baggy shorts that look like a skirt," I said.

"Culottes," Agent Atkin said. "They look like something they're not."

"Like the Chameleon," I said.

"She was charming us," Sam said.

"To get us to reveal info," I said.

"That's how come we told her we're rich," Sam said.

"You're rich?" Agent Atkin said.

"Kid rich," I said. "Not adult rich.

"I have fifty-six dollars and sixty-eight cents in my life savings account," I told her. "Sam has forty-two bucks and thirty-six cents."

"But she thinks we're child millionaires," Sam said.

"Is that all the 'evidence'?" Agent Atkin asked.

"Nope," I said. "She lives on Eighth Street."

"Agent Atkin," Sam said. "Shouldn't you be writing this down?"

She poked the side of her head. "I'm keeping everything you said right here. Instant recall."

"Another clue," Sam said. "She smells good."

"Like perfume?" Agent Atkin said.

"Like bacon," Sam said.

"Good to know," Agent Atkin said. "Thank you for bringing this to our attention."

"Throw down a dragnet fast," I said. "She's probably out mail-frauding right now."

"I'll tell my supervisor," Agent Atkin said.

"We have a confession," I said.

She sat down.

"When we met the Chameleon we didn't know she was an MW," Sam said.

"We told her confidential FBI information," I admitted.

"What information?" Agent Atkin asked.

"About how the FBI can test hair for DNA that will lead straight to the criminal," I said.

"And we told about the FATS academy," Sam said.

"Do we have to turn in our badges?" I asked.

Her look was serious. All I could think was *Goodbye, my sweet career*.

"That information is not classified," she said.

"Really?" I said.

"What a relief!" Sam said.

"I recommend you stop telling the public," I said. "Some of them are crooks."

Agent Atkin smiled, stood up, and buttoned her blue jacket.

"Good work, men," she said. "We'll take it from here."

It feels great to do your duty.

"What's your phone number?" I asked. "In case we get more information."

"Or ideas," Sam said.

"Now, that IS classified," she said.

*   *   *

We sat in the back of the Metro car, behind the plastic divider so we'd be more soundproof.

"The Chameleon has to be C and C from my mother," I said. "Classified and Confidential."

"What about your dad?" Sam asked.

"My dad says that the only secrets married people should keep are birthday presents," I said. "He can't know either. It's for their own protection."

"What about my parents?" Sam asked.

"Keep mum, Chum," I said. "Especially around your mom. She has told my mom things before."

"I can't believe how nice she seemed," Sam said.

"Your mom IS nice," I said. "She has to tell my mom stuff. It's the Code of Mothers."

"I know my mother is nice, Melonhead," he said. "I'm talking about the Chameleon."

After supper my dad called from Pensacola.

"Mom sure is happy tonight," he said. "I hear you had a smooth day."

"Smooth as a two-by-four," I said. "Nothing broke. Nothing spilled. No concussions. No stitches. Nothing important got lost. Nobody called Mom to report on me. And Sam and I did not get into a single situation."

"You know what Mom calls those days?" my dad asked.

"All too rare," I said.

That is a man-to-man joke.

"Stick to the Guidelines, Sport. I'd like the same good news when I call tomorrow."

I was in the kitchen, building a salami and ketchup tower to take up to my room for a midnight snack, when I got one of my all-time great ideas.

I hid the stacked salami in the bread box. Then I put the pointy ketchup top up my nose and squeezed. Then I exhaled through my nostrils like a mad horse. Ketchup dripped down and around my lips. I lay on the floor. I rolled my eyes so far back that only the whites showed. Then I called out, "Mom, come take my picture!" I let my tongue flap to the side.

My mom came in screaming. "You're bleeding like a stuck pig! What happened? I'm calling your father."

"Mom," I said.

She mashed a dishtowel against my nose.

"Don't talk. Save your strength," she said. "And try not to bleed on the floor."

I almost burst from laughing.

"It's ketchup," I said.

"That's not funny. You frightened me."

"I wasn't trying to scare you," I said. "I wanted you to take my picture. I'm sending it to Lucy Rose at camp."

"Is that a kind thing to do?" my mom asked.

She answered her own question. "It is not."

"Come on, Mom," I begged. "She'll think it's hilarious."

"She's an odd girl," my mom said.

"That's the best thing about her," I said.

My mom smiled.

"Stop thinking

that," I said. "She's a girl and she's my friend and that's all. Period."

My mom left the room.

"It's a waste of ketchup if you don't take the picture," I yelled.

She came back with her camera. I made my tongue go limp.

"It's the best photo ever taken," I said. "Thanks."

"I don't understand you," my mom said. "But I do love you."

4
ON THE CASE

Luckily for Sam and me and unluckily for the Chameleon, my mom had to drive to Baltimore first thing this morning. She was taking my aunt to the doctor. She thinks her eyes are making her look old. My aunt's eyes, not my mom's. I don't know how she expects a doctor to fix that.

I got dropped off at Sam's with a mile of instructions.

"Be polite. Stay out of trouble," my mom said. "Don't eat them out of house and home."

"It's too hot to breathe or cook," Sam's mom said. "I'm sending them to Baking Divas for lunch."

"Don't play with anything sharp," my mom told me. "And help out with Baby Julia."

"Don't worry, Betty," Mrs. Alswang said.

"Wuwee, Bedy," Julia said.

My mom drove off.

"Make a healthy choice at the Divas," Mrs. Alswang told us. "Charge your lunches to our account."

Account means you don't pay until you get a bill at the end of the month. We have an account too. I don't get to use it, due to the time I charged a Supreme Seven-Layer Caramel Cake without permission.

"Thanks, Mom," Sam said.

"Where are you going after lunch?" Mrs. Alswang asked.

That's when Sam's brain had a nuclear meltdown.

"We're following the Chameleon," he said.

I socked him in the back. Hard. It made him cough.

Mrs. Alswang laughed. "You have a better

chance of finding a leprechaun on Capitol Hill than a chameleon."

"Camel un," Julia said.

"You're right, Mrs. Alswang," I said. "There's zero chance of finding a chameleon this far north."

On the skateboard ride to Divas we took a break to buy Warheads. Then we sat on the Congress Market bench and ate them.

"I blurted 'Chameleon' without thinking," Sam said. "Good save."

"You have to remember when we're undercover," I said. "That was a last-second escape."

I pulled my old Cursive Practice book out of my backpack. "I brought an Evidence Log," I said. "I stopped practicing cursive after the Gs, so there's plenty of paper. I taped our toilet paper notes to the new page one."

"The cover's sticky," Sam said.

"It was under my bed when my secret stash of grape jelly leaked," I said. "But I cleaned it with spit."

Sam rubbed the Log on his shorts.

"I brought my entire golf pencil collection," I said.

"Anything else?"

"The telescope I got for my birthday. My life-guard whistle. Pockets full of cereal, of course."

"Did you bring the handcuffs?" Sam asked.

"My dad had to unhinge the plastic when I locked myself to the radiator and toasted my arm," I said.

Sam unzipped his backpack. "Presenting my mom's camera," he said. "If we bust it, we're dead."

"Why would we bust it?" I asked.

"We wouldn't," he said. "I also brought one rope, water, two bungee cords, and Scotch tape to put on our fingers. That way, no prints."

"That is a lifesaver of an idea," I said.

Sam put a bungee cord through the camera strap and wrapped it around his middle, for a belt.

"E-Z P-Z, rice and cheezie," I said.

We were skateboarding across North Carolina Avenue when Sam yelled, "Does tracking the Chameleon go against your Guidelines?"

"The opposite. G for L number six. We're taking personal responsibility for our country."

"I meant number four," Sam said.

"Ask an Adult? That's only if you're wondering if it's a bad idea. I'm not wondering. Are you?"

"Nope," he said.

"Not much danger in surveilling," I said.

"True," Sam said.

"We could ask Mrs. Wilkins," I said. "Just in case."

We met Mrs. Wilkins by accident. I threw a ball that busted her plant.

"She's so old she's like having two adults," Sam said.

"Plus she has wisdom," I said. "Also I'm interested in her new fake hip."

5

MRS. WILKINS AND THE BONE SAW

We opened Mrs. Wilkins's door with the key from under the mat. I'm allowed.

I yelled at top volume. "Hello! It's us, Melon-head and Sam."

Mrs. Wilkins's daughter, Molly, came running out of the kitchen with her finger on her lips. "Shhh! Mom's sleeping."

Mrs. Wilkins told me that Molly is bossy for a thirty-three-year-old.

"I'm not asleep," Mrs. Wilkins yelled. "I'm trapped in the living room."

We stood by the hall table. It's made of jungle wood. Mrs. Wilkins was in the lazy chair

that used to be her husband's. He's dead so now it's hers.

"I hope you're not expecting me to come to you," Mrs. Wilkins said.

"We're not," Sam said.

We walked across the living room rug and stopped on the new-hip side.

"How's your gaping wound?" I asked.

"My gaping wound is my own business," she said.

"That's her pain talking," Molly said. "Mom doesn't mean to act like that."

"She's not acting," I said. "She's always a crab."

Both of them laughed.

"It's polite to bring sick people a present," Mrs. Wilkins said.

"Nobody told me that," I said.

"I just did," she said.

"How many stitches did you get?" Sam asked.

"Two hundred thirty-seven," Mrs. Wilkins said. "I told the doctor you'd want to know."

"You have the luck!" I said. "That's more than all of mine added up."

"Stitches are interesting," Sam said.

"I'll give you interesting," Mrs. Wilkins said. "I got to hold my hip in my hand."

"Your real hip or your fake hip?" I asked.

"Fake," she said. "Before they installed it."

"What does it look like?" Sam asked.

"Picture a big Tootsie Roll Pop," she said. "After

they sawed off my worn-out bone, they put the stick in my thigh bone and the ball in the socket."

"Is it like a Ping-Pong ball or a tennis ball?" I asked.

"Closer to a Ping-Pong ball," she said.

"Did the doctor use a power saw to cut your bones?"

"She said she did," Mrs. Wilkins said. "She also went at me with a drill."

"Why?" Sam said.

"How else would she get the screws in?"

"Screws?" Sam said.

"Of course screws," I told him. "So her new hip won't fall apart when she's jumping."

"Was the drill like Pop's?" Sam asked.

"Cleaner, I hope," Mrs. Wilkins said.

"Man-o-man alive," I said. "They should have taken a movie. People would pay us money to watch it."

"Us?" Mrs. Wilkins said. "It's my hip. I'd say it's my money."

"Is your new hip made of plastic?" Sam asked.

"Titanium," she said.

"Actual titanium from meteorites and moon rocks?" I asked.

"My titanium is probably from a more local source," she said.

"Maybe not," I said. "You could be walking around with moon rock for a hip."

"That is one strong hip," Sam told her. "They use titanium to make missiles and airplanes."

"And hips," she said.

"I bet you'll turn bionic!" I said. "Titanium is as strong as steel and lighter than aluminum. It survives extreme hot and below-zero cold. If you got all your bones replaced with titanium you'd be unstoppable."

"Do you want to hear or do you want to interrupt?" she asked.

"Hear," I said.

"Okay," she said. "Soon enough, new bone is going to surround it and take over."

"Man, I hope I get a fake hip when I'm old," I said.

"I hope you don't," she said.

That was ungenerous.

"Think you'll ever invent something as clever as a hip?" Mrs. Wilkins asked.

"Probably cleverer," I said.

Molly laughed.

I told them about my mortal wound photo. "Want Sam to take a picture of you drooling ketchup, Mrs. Wilkins? You could mail it to your sons."

"That's an appealing idea," she said.

"It's an appalling idea," Molly said. "I can't think of a more disgusting idea than lying around with a mouthful of ketchup."

"I can think of over a hundred things," Sam said.

"I've personally seen Bart Bigelow put nose pickings in his mouth," I said. "Ketchup would be nothing to him."

"No good comes from comparing yourself to a nose-picker," Mrs. Wilkins said. "Remember that."

"Okay," I said. "Compare me to Sam. He loves jokes. He loves ketchup."

"My sister tries to drink it out of the bottle," Sam said.

"That's no surprise," Mrs. Wilkins said. "The last time I saw Baby Julia, she was licking a cat."

Mrs. Wilkins was starting to look dozy. Molly was hanging around wiping dust off the fertile statue. Mrs. Wilkins got it in Africa.

"My mom would never let a naked statue in our house," I said.

Sam leaned over Mrs. Wilkins's head and whispered into her hearing aid. "We need to ask you a private question."

"Scram, Molly," Mrs. Wilkins said.

"Two minutes, boys," Molly said. "Mom needs rest."

"Talk fast," Mrs. Wilkins said. "She won't stay gone long."

"Guess what we did yesterday?" Sam said.

"Did it involve the rescue squad?" she asked.

"Not this time," I told her. "It involves the FBI and a lady fugitive."

"Begin with the fugitive," she said.

We ended with Agent Atkin. Mrs. Wilkins laughed quite a few times. That was the medicine talking.

By the end, her eyes were drooping.

I poked her shoulder. Sam said, "What do you think, Mrs. Wilkins?"

"Keep up the good work," she said.

"Don't worry," I said. "We will."

"Next time you come, remember my present."

6
FIVE-STAR BAKERY

"Next stop: lunch at Baking Divas," Sam said. "I'm nearly dead from starvation."

Splitting my pocket full of Corn Pops only helped a little. Handing off cereal while you're skateboarding downhill at fifty or more miles an hour, you can't help having some fly-aways.

At the exact time we got there, G for L number three came into my head.

"Consider Consequences," Sam said. "With a MWFFJ on the loose, we have to break our habit of leaving our skateboards in front of the Divas' door."

"If the Chameleon spots them she'll swipe them," I said.

"Not if we jam them in the space between the Divas' flower box and the brick wall," Sam said. "Like this."

"Uh-oh!" I said. "Dirt avalanche!"

"Can you believe Mr. McBee built boxes that tip over when they're barely touched?" Sam said.

"G for L number one," I said. "Mr. McBee caused the Flower Box Nosedive Effect. Mrs. McBee is going to be ticked with him."

"Not if we pick it up fast," he said.

"Luckily, the dirt clumps busted up when the box hit the ground," I said. "That makes replanting super-speedy."

Inside Baking Divas, there was a customer backup. People had to take Now Serving numbers. Mine was sixty-seven.

I also took sixty-eight and sixty-nine.

Sam grabbed seventy through seventy-three. "You can have my extras for your collection," he said.

"Melonhead and Sam. Give those extra numbers to the customers behind you," Aunt Frankie said. "And leave that machine alone."

Jonique was behind the gigantic marble table, folding bakery boxes. Mrs. McBee won't hire me to work behind the counter, even for free. When I told Pop he said, "Mothers tend to favor their children. That's a fact of life."

"Hey, Jonique," I yelled.

She waved her arms like a five-speed fan and ran to the counter. "Hey, Melonhead! Hey, Sam! Have a free Five-Star Snicker-doodle."

"Don't yell it," I said. "Everybody will want one."

"Everybody gets one," she said. "It's a reward because Baking Divas got to be in the *Hill Rag*."

"The *Food Revue* called us a neighborhood treasure and a five-star bakery," Mrs. McBee said.

"Did they put the Divas' pictures in the story?" Sam asked.

"No," Jonique said. "And it's a good thing,

because Aunt Frankie says they've been cooking so hard they look like hags."

"They're not that haggish," I said.

"And you are not that annoying," Aunt Frankie said.

"Thank you," I said. "Did you hear that, Jonique? We're not that annoying."

"See? You were wrong about us," Sam told Jonique. "Admit it."

She wouldn't.

"Well done, ladies," Mr. Wagner said. "J. A. Fischer rarely gives anyone five stars."

"Except us," Aunt Frankie said.

She was in one of her dancing moods.

"I promised Jeremiah and Kendall we'd get Cinni-minis," Mrs. Washington told her. "But I also want to buy whatever J. A. Fischer liked best, boxed to go."

The Divas call that BTG.

"He said the only thing better than a Co-Co-Nutty-Buddy is two Co-Co-Nutty-Buddies," Jonique said.

Mrs. McBee read, "'. . . an explosion of chewiness

with molasses and caramel undertones that have been mellowed by a good deal of butter.'"

"Mr. Fisher is the number one restaurant critic in this city, but he didn't guess the secret ingredient," Aunt Frankie said.

"What is it?" Sam asked.

"A secret," Mrs. McBee said.

"I'll take a dozen," Mrs. Hackett said. She was number sixty-nine, thanks to me.

"Coming up," Jonique told her. She was standing on the wooden box her dad built so she could reach over the cake case. It makes customers think she's taller than Sam and me.

Number seventy-three yelled from the back of the line. "Lola and Frankie, you are two great businesswomen!"

"We're grateful businesswomen," Mrs. McBee yelled back. "Sales have doubled since we got our stars. I had to get Jonique to come in to box Tasha Tudor Tortes. And a lady in Portland, Oregon, read about our Monumental Cookies and called in for four dozen! We've never had a mail order before."

"Shouldn't five stars mean we get five free cookies?" I asked.

"I'm thankful that you are not my child," Mrs. McBee said. "You'd eat us right out of business."

All the ladies laughed.

"Today we're eating you INTO business," Sam said. "My mom said we can sign for lunch."

The new thing at Divas is Sandwiches from Around the World.

"Want Cracker Jacks?" Jonique asked.

"For lunch?" Mr. Meany said.

"They're not sweet," Jonique told him. "They're Diva-made crackers with pepper-jack cheese."

"And jalapeño peppers if you want them, which I do," I said.

"Which country are Cracker Jacks from?" Mr. Meany asked.

"America," Jonique said. "Because I invented them."

They're pretty big so I only got two.

"I'm deciding between an empanada from Argentina and a crêpe from France," Sam said.

The only other choice of the day was Thai

Lettuce Wraps. My mom loves them because they have lettuce instead of bread. That's the same reason Sam and I don't.

"Empanada, please," Sam said.

We both got chocolate milk and You're a Star cookies.

It took us under six minutes to eat.

"Don't leave before you tell me if you can make a delivery for us," Mrs. McBee said.

"Is it BTG?" I asked.

"And waiting," Mrs. McBee said.

"We still get paid in cookies, right?" Sam said.

"Double cookies today," she said. "I'm desperate."

"I'll take mine in Two-Tone Twists and Nutella Knots," I said.

"Ditto," Sam told her.

Aunt Frankie handed two boxes and six cookies over the counter.

"They go to the

Capitol Hill Retirement Home," she said. "No charge for the day-olds. The second box is a Three Kings Cake for Mrs. Bazoo. She works at the front desk."

"We know Mrs. Bazoo," I said.

"Her cake is a special order," Mrs. McBee said. "The best I could promise was that I'd get it to her one day this week. If she's off today, leave it with the cookies at the front desk."

"What's Three Kings Cake?" I asked.

"A less creative person would call it spice," Mrs. McBee said.

"But a less creative person wouldn't replace sugar with honey and doll it up with marzipan flowers," Aunt Frankie said.

"I never knew what kings ate," I said. "But if I was one, I'd add chocolate chips."

"When you become a king I'll change the recipe," Mrs. McBee said. "Until then, get going."

We ate our reward cookies outside.

"Problem," Sam said. "We can't surveil the Chameleon and deliver at the same time."

"You deliver," I said. "I'll stake out. Come to Eighth Street when you're done."

"FBI rule number one is Never Work Alone," Sam said.

"I know," I said. "If one person gets captured, one has to be left to report to the Bureau."

"We should have told Mrs. McBee we were too busy," Sam said.

"I got carried away by free food," I said.

Sam held the cookie box by the string. "You busted G for L number two. Plan Ahead."

"True, but we're helping a desperate woman," I said. "That's G for L number nine. Think of Others."

"I say we surveil now. Deliver on the way home," Sam said.

"It's a deal, Banana Peel."

7
UP A TREE

Sam and I skateboarded through the walking alley that connects Seventh Street to Eighth.

"When we get to the end, it's telescope time," I said. "I'll be the looker."

"Flatten yourself against the brick wall," Sam said. "Creep your head around the corner. That way, most of you is out of sight. I'll be the observation recorder."

10:26 a.m. There are three houses with red doors. One house has a tower and a green window.

"We have to get closer," Sam said.

"I'll crawl on the sidewalk and through the tree

boxes," I told him. "The parked cars will be my wall of protection."

"If the coast is clear, act like you're yawning."

"Too obvious," I said. "I'll pretend I'm catching a fly."

Two minutes later I was crouching behind a red Toyota and grabbing air.

Sam got there in a flash. "See that pin oak? It's big. It has a view of the Chameleon's house."

Luckily it was trash day. Recycle cans were still on the curb. I frog-walked one over to the back of the tree.

Sam climbed up and dropped rope. I tied on our backpacks and the Divas boxes. Sam reeled them in.

Once I shinnied up, we

set up the surveillance station. "We're made in the shade, Jade," I said. "Camouflaged by leaves."

"I bungee-corded the Divas boxes on that high branch for safety," Sam said.

"Good work, Agent Alswang," I said. "What do you see through the telescope?"

"Lots of usual things," he said. "But no action at the Chameleon's house."

11:17 a.m. Nothing.

"Surveilling is not as interesting as it looks on TV," Sam said.

"It would be better if we had a pizza truck with one-way windows and zoom cameras," I said. "And air-conditioning. Plus a fridge."

"We'd have to move at rush hour," Sam said.

"Even better," I said. "We'd learn to drive."

"Stop the clock!" Sam said. "A lady is coming out!"

"The Chameleon?"

"False alarm," Sam said. "This lady has

mouse-colored hair and her shoulders are bent forward. Her weight is slender."

11:31 a.m. Lady. Mouse hair. Skinny. Hunched.

"Write this down," Sam said.

Tan shirt with wavy fabric in front. Sleeves. Baggy black skirt. Shoes are Band-Aid color.

"Why is she wearing old-lady shoes?" I asked.

"Because she's old," Sam said.

"Maybe she's the Chameleon's mom," I said.

"The MW report didn't say anything about a mother," Sam said.

"It said family," I said. "Mothers are family."

"A man is walking up the street. She's waving at him. He's not so old."

"The accomplice!"

"They're going inside," Sam said.

"Let me see."

I took over on the telescope, but nothing else happened until the disaster.

"What's that scratching?" Sam asked.

I looked up.

"Oh, brother!" I said.

It was a squirrel. He was standing on top of a Divas box. He had a Cherry Blossom cookie in his paws. There was a bite missing.

"Another one is behind you," Sam said. "I mean three more."

"This is bad," I told Sam. "Once a squirrel gets an idea, he tells the others. The next thing you know, you're living in Squirreltown."

"I didn't know that," he said.

"I have squirrel experience," I said. "Believe me."

I blew four quick blasts on my whistle.

Cookie Squirrel let go of the Cherry Blossom. One of her brothers raced down the trunk and pounced on it.

The rest of the pack surrounded the white box. Two were gnawing their way in.

"They're probably starving," Sam said.

"Pop says city squirrels are

never starving," I said. "They just like eating. Squirrels and I are alike that way."

"That fat gray one is trying to get his head in the hole," Sam said.

I threw a handful of cereal up in the air.

"Pay attention, squirrels," Sam said. "It's raining Chocolate Cheerios."

Cookie Squirrel zipped past my face. The others ran after him.

To keep the squirrel parade on the ground, I had to drop cereal bits every hundred seconds.

Nothing, except squirrel feeding, happened until

12:49 p.m. Upstairs window shade went up. Could be a signal.

12:50 p.m. Second shade up.

The man and lady coming outside. Opening the gate. Walking toward the Metro.

"Should we follow them?" Sam asked.

"No," I said. "The Chameleon probably sent her mother out for a distraction in case she's being watched by the FBI."

"Which she is," Sam said.

"Criminal minds are sneaky but sharp," I said.

By two o'clock I was so hungry I could have fallen out of the tree.

"Maybe we could eat one of the old people's cookies," Sam said.

"I don't think the retired would miss two," I said.

"If they knew we're working for the FBI they would probably say help yourself," Sam said.

"They'd appreciate that we're helping our country," I said.

I stood up and wiggled my hand through the gnawed hole in the Divas box.

"If there's a Sweetie Pie, I want it," Sam said.

"Sam, the box is over my head and tied shut. I'm like the Magic Claw game at the diner. What I grab is what I grab."

My first pick turned out to be a Coffee Toffee Bar. The second was an Orange Gina cupcake. I split them and put two halves on Sam's branch. He handed me the telescope.

"Throw down some Apple Jacks," he said. "Squirrels can hear when you're eating."

Sam watched nothing happen. "Do you think two more cookies would matter?"

"Sending up the Magic Claw," I said in my robot voice.

Sam reached across the leaves to collect his Monumental Cookie and Blue Moon.

"Superb, Herb," he said.

I gave him a broken Choc-O-Lot.

"Fill your belly, Nellie."

2:09 p.m. Mailman.

I dangled my legs so the blood wouldn't drain out of my feet. Then I situated my butt.

"This is more boring than standing in line," Sam said.

"More boring than clothes shopping," I said.

"More boring than Mrs. Washburn talking about adverbs."

"More boring than an infomercial starring Mrs. Washburn talking about adverbs," I said.

"Boring times infinity," Sam said.

"Dullness multiplies when you're hungry."

"The Return of the Magic Claw," Sam said.

"Jackpot!" I said. "A hunk of Lola's Lively Lemon Cake. It got shaved coming through the squirrel hole, but it's tasty."

"Switcheroo," Sam said. "I'll be in charge of the Log and the Retired Cookies."

4:00 p.m. Old lady is back. No accomplice. Suspicious behavior: Looking around before unlocking door.

"Where did she go?" Sam asked.

"Maybe to the doctor," I said. "She's walking smoother than before."

5:11 p.m. Nothing for over 1 hour.

"When do stakeouts end?" Sam asked.

"Six o'clock," I said. "You take the scope. My eyeball feels wrinkled."

Then luck struck.

"Door opening," Sam said. "Lady legs coming through."

Yellow hair. Not old. Orange shorts. Shirt is color of swimming pool water.

"It's the Chameleon!" he said.

"Watch her like ten hawks," I said.

"You wouldn't think an MW would bother with watering plants," Sam said.

"When you're sly like she's sly, you ask yourself,

What do regular people do? Then you do it," I said. "The next thing we know she'll be buying avocados."

5:49 p.m. The Chameleon back inside.

"My butt can't take any more," I said.

"I have petrified legs," Sam said.

"Unbend, my friend," I said.

I hugged the biggest branch and let my body swing in the air. "Lowering for a landing," I said.

"On your butt," Sam said. "The can's gone."

"Gone where?"

"Somebody moved it," he said.

"With no warning?" I said.

"What if I hadn't noticed?" Sam said. "It would be their fault that your legs snapped in two."

"I'm slipping," I said.

I landed on what Sam predicted.

"Bark burn?" Sam asked.

"Wrists to armpits," I said.

"Better than butt breakage," Sam laughed.

"Or a butt cast," I hooted.

"Stand by for supplies," Sam said.

"Hurry," I said. "If the Chameleon sees us, we're throttled."

I borrowed back the trash can. Our lowering system worked well for Sam. Ditto for the backpacks. For Mrs. Bazoo's cake, not at all.

8

CAKE MISTAKE

"Just dust off the halves and push them back together," I said. "Once it's back in the box, we'll smooth the icing with our fingers and pick off the mulch."

"There's crumbling going on," Sam said.

"Give it to me. I can do it," I told him.

"We'll both do it," he said.

"That's a lot of icing on your shirt," I said.

"I'll lick it off later," Sam said.

I wrinkled my forehead so he could read my thought.

"Fine," he said. "You can lick half of my shirt."

"Thank you."

"First we make a plate with our hands," he said. "On the count of three, bend over. Then lift."

It worked for a split of a split second.

"Freeze!" Sam yelled. "A new crack is starting."

"It's like the cake's unzipping," I said.

"Unzipped," he said. "Chunks are falling on my sneakers."

"Get the box!"

"Too late! Hold the pieces like cups. Icing side down," Sam said. "Catch the sliding layer."

He did. With his arm.

"I'll get it!" I said, and picked the hunk up with my teeth.

"What else could I do?" I asked.

"Is it good?" Sam asked.

"Tremendous,"
I said.

We plopped
Sam's half and
my quarters in
the box.

"We'll just remold it," I said.

"The sides are covered with handprints," Sam said.

We looked at the cake from every direction.

"Is there anything to do but eat it?" I asked.

"Throw it away," Sam said. "But that would be a waste."

When we finished, I wiped my hands on the back of my shorts.

"You can have all your shirt icing," I said.

"There's cake on your eyebrow," I told him.

"And your cheeks," he said.

"My stomach is stirred up," I said.

"From the cake?" Sam asked.

"Not from eating it, from thinking about eating it."

"And ruining it," he said. "And not delivering it."

"It was a freak accident," I said.

"Remember the time in front of the cake case?" Sam asked. "When our thumb wrestling turned into a pushing match?"

"Aunt Frankie was steaming mad," I said.

"She'll be madder about this," he said.

"We're in trouble, Barney Rubble," I said.

"At least the cookies are fine," Sam said.

"But the box looks bad," I said. "Especially the eaten part."

"Put the cookies in the cake box," Sam said. "It's only a little bashed."

I untied the string. Sam pulled up the lid.

"Four cookies?" I screamed. "How can that be?"

"Those squirrels were pigs," Sam said.

"Or we were," I said.

"This is a shock," Sam said.

"Like getting hit in the face with a fish," I said.

"You've been hit in the face with a fish?" Sam asked.

"Only once."

"We flunked G for L number nine," he said. "Think of Others."

"Number nine gets canceled out by number five," I said.

"Right!" Sam said. "All we have to do is fix this mistake!"

9

NO PROBLEM

Sam and I met at Jimmy T's right after breakfast.
I ordered Dr Pepper and orange soda mixed. Sam
was so depressed he got plain Sprite. Luckily, I had
a brainiac attack.

"Mrs. Wilkins!" I shouted.

We stopped at Jonny and Joon's corner store on
the way.

"Can you eat Twizzlers with fake teeth?" I asked.

"Maybe not," Jonny said.

"Go with soft," Joon said.

Molly was sitting on the porch when we got
there.

"Mom doesn't have much energy yet," she said.

Mrs. Wilkins yelled, "I believe that being inside my body, as in fact I am, makes me a better judge of how I feel."

"That's the problem with open windows," Molly told us.

"I heard that," Mrs. Wilkins shouted.

Sam pressed his nose against the screen.

"Is your hearing aid turned to maximum?" Sam asked.

"Come inside, boys."

Sam plopped down on the living room floor. I sat on the sofa arm.

"Stop fidgeting," Mrs. Wilkins said.

"You are one hundred percent better looking," I told her.

"Does your new hip feel younger than your old hip?" Sam asked.

"So far, it feels like a pain in the hip," Mrs. Wilkins said.

"Here's your gift," I said. "Sorry it's mashed."

"Three Musketeers!" she said. "Maybe I'll have surgery more often."

"You could be a volunteer for doctors who need to practice," I said.

She shoved the candy bar under her pillow. "Molly only approves of protein and whole grains," she said.

"If I tried to boss my mom I would be in octuple trouble," I said. "Believe me."

"She calls it being efficient," Mrs. Wilkins said. "But I'll admit she makes good soft-boiled eggs."

"I bet you miss hospital food," I said.

"Not at all," she said.

"Are you kidding? It's a life dream of mine to eat hospital food," I said.

"It's a dream if you like butter pats on paper squares and Jell-O three times a day."

"We do like that," Sam said.

"Hey," I said. "Has any gross stuff leaked out of the gaping wound?"

"Sorry to disappoint," Mrs. Wilkins said. "It's done up with ointment and gauze to keep infection away."

Molly came through the pocket doors that lead to the dining room. "I'm going to Roland's for a loaf of bread and eggs," she said.

"And ice cream," Mrs. Wilkins said.

I waited until the front door closed.

"We're in a situation," I said.

Sam told about the cookies first. Then I explained the cake.

"Can you tell us what we should do about it?" Sam asked.

"I can," Mrs. Wilkins said. "But I won't."

"You won't?" I asked.

"I didn't eat the cake," she said.

We sat like two lumps.

"I do have a small idea," Mrs. Wilkins said. "Do you have the four uneaten cookies?"

"They're in Melonhead's backpack," Sam said.

"Give them to me," Mrs. Wilkins said.

We turned over two Jiggy Figgy Bars, one Nutella Knot, and one Smart Blondie.

"Now what?" I asked.

"Now you can honestly say that you gave cookies to a retired person."

Sam and I rode our
bikes to the Capitol.
After ten minutes of
lying on the grass,
looking at the
sky, and waving
away gnats, I said,
"The cookies were
day-old."

"Day-old is not as good as fresh,"
Sam said.

"Mrs. McBee gives them to the retired for free,"
I said.

"It's like they're worthless," Sam said.

"Lucy Rose got to eat in the Retirement Home
dining room once," I said. "She told me it's sweet
city. They have honey buns for breakfast. Cupcakes
for lunch. Pies for dinner. Ice cream whenever they
want. It's like they live in the game of Candy Land."

"The last thing the old need is a box of day-olds,"
Sam said.

"It's not like they were expecting cookies," I said.

"They just turn up whenever Mrs. McBee has an overload," Sam said.

"I say we forget about the cookies," I said. "No harm. No foul."

"No problem," Sam said.

Except for the cake.

10
SUNDAE FRIDAY

We found Baby Julia smearing snot on the Alswangs' living room wall.

"I pannin," Julia said.

Sam and I taught her that. I mean, not to smear snot on walls. We taught her to paint. Actually, she taught herself but we were the ones who got blamed.

"Hello, Sam!" Mrs. Alswang called out.

"Melonhead is with me," Sam yelled.

"Hello, Melonhead," Sam's mom yelled.

"Hello, Mrs. Alswang," I yelled back.

"Can you check on Julia?" she hollered.

"She's fine," Sam yelled. "Just sitting on the living room floor."

"Can you bring her to me?"

I carried Julia upstairs to Mrs. Alswang's office. Sam carried Julia's blanket. It also had a considerable amount of snot on it.

Julia pointed. "Bewenhid."

"She knows my name!" I said.

"You're an important person in her life," Sam's mom said. "You make her laugh."

I felt good about that.

"Bewenhid?" Julia said.

"I am so pleased with you guys," Sam's mom said. "The Guidelines have helped you both."

"True," I said.

Not counting the cake situation.

"From now on the Melon Family G for Ls are also the Alswang G for Ls," she said. "Adam's mom is making us a poster. And to celebrate all this goodness, Adam is invited to spend the night. I'm making a special dinner. And we're going to Madam and Pop's for Sidewalk Sundaes. Your mom's meeting us there with your overnight gear, Adam."

Dinner was called root vegetables. Luckily, it came with hot dogs.

Lucy Rose's mom was already at Madam and Pop's. She's their daughter. She gets to come over whenever she wants.

Mrs. Reilly hugged the skin off us.

"I haven't seen you guys since Lucy Rose left for camp," she said. "I wonder if she's growing as fast as you two."

"She's probably so tall you won't recognize her," I said.

Her face drooped.

I made a triple-decker chocolate mint, strawberry, rocky road cone. In between scoops I put mashed cherries. Then I squirted four inches of whipped cream on top. I also squirted some down the back of Sam's shirt.

Sam stirred coffee, peach, and chocolate mint ice creams together until they were soft. Then he added Marshmallow Fluff and a load of sprinkles. He dumped another load down the back of my pants.

Madam said we have a flair. "Do you like to cook?" she asked.

"I'm not allowed," I told her.

"His mom has Fear of Mess," Sam said.

Sam's dad took pictures of Julia washing her face with chocolate syrup. Mrs. Reilly took pictures of Sam and me with whipped-cream eyebrows. She's sending them to Lucy Rose. Then we had feet fights in the hammock. Sam and me. Not me and Mrs. Reilly.

My mom brought my Spider-Man suitcase. It's from when I was five years old. She and Madam talked until the fireflies started blinking. It was probably about me. Madam is a child expert. My mom's always asking her if I'm coming out right.

Madam and Pop's rule is Kids Clean Up. Madam hangs around the kitchen.

"Do you know how to make Three Kings Cake?" Sam asked.

"I've never heard of it," Madam said.

"Uncreative people call it spice," I said.

"Spice cake is Pop's favorite," Madam said. "Can you reach that red book on the top shelf?"

"Who knew there's such a thing as an all-dessert cookbook?" I said.

"Life is good," Madam said.

"Can we borrow it?" I asked. "We need it to cook a cake. Privately."

"How interesting," Madam said. "Do you have a private kitchen?"

"Your kitchen is private," Sam said.

"It's available tomorrow," she said.

"Can't," I said. "We have a job."

"I have a meeting tomorrow night," Madam said. "But if it's okay with your parents, Pop might be game for a cake adventure."

"Oh, he will be," Sam said. "Pop loves a project."

"My mom thinks I have the habit of inviting myself," I said.

"Would it help if I ask if you can come over?" Madam said.

"A lot," I said. "Don't say why. It's a secret cake."

Madam smiled like we were doing something great. "I have everything you need," she said.

"We're using honey instead of sugar," Sam said. "Plus we need a marzipan."

"I have honey," Madam said. "The marzipan is your job."

Sam and I stayed up past midnight turning his bottom bunk bed into a Junior Special Agent office.

"First thing tomorrow we go to your house and pick up our periscope," Sam said.

Since I was the guest, I got to sleep on the floor.

11
FROG LEGS

Mrs. Alswang thinks kids have a load of time to do work for adults. Luckily, her chores are action packed. We're not allowed to wash the car anymore. I say wax for cars should be called car wax. Wax for floors should be called some other name. Like Shiner. Then nobody would get them mixed up.

Since it was Saturday, Mr. Alswang was off taking photos of a wedding. Sam and I had to watch Julia. She was combing the rug with a fork.

"I'm paying a penny a dandelion," Mrs. Alswang said. "A dime if the roots are attached."

"Sorry," Sam said to me. "I'm not allowed to turn down chores. Even the free ones."

"Speed-weed!" I whispered. "The Chameleon's waiting."

"Julia's copying us," I told Mrs. Alswang. "Only she's pulling up pansies."

We replanted. Mrs. Alswang did the weed count. "One dollar and forty-two cents," she said.

"Not bad considering all but seven were rootless," I said.

"Luckily, we had a lot of weeds for a city yard," Sam said.

"If we were weeding my old yard in Florida, we'd be thousandaires by now," I told Sam.

Mrs. Alswang laughed.

"Mom," Sam said. "Julia's trying to stretch an earthworm."

Too late.

"Don't worry," I said. "The head end will live."

"Not in your mouth, sweetie!" Mrs. Alswang said.

"I wish you could talk better, Julia," I said. "I always wanted to know what raw worm tastes like."

When we finally got excused we ran to my

house. My dad was sitting on the porch swing, fanning himself with a pizza flyer.

"Hello, Sport. Hello, Sam."

"You're home!" I said.

"And happy to be here," my dad said. "I flew in this morning. I hear you've been superglue on Guidelines."

"What?" Sam asked.

"I stuck to them," I said. "Like you told me on the phone, Dad. The right thing is not always the easy thing."

"We aren't an easy-thing family, Sport. For us it's the right thing or nothing. That's the Code of the Melons."

"Sometimes the right thing is a scary thing," Sam said.

He was thinking about the Chameleon.

"It can be," my dad said. "But we Melons are a brave people."

"Ditto the Alswangs," Sam said.

"I'm not asking if you brought me a present from Florida," I said. "But I am wondering."

He handed me a key chain with a plastic shark floating in real water in a fake ice cube. On top it said The Sunshine State.

"It's for your collection," my dad said.

"I was hoping for money," I told him.

"The money from Florida is the same money we use in Washington, D.C.," he said.

"I know," I said.

"When did you go money mad?" he asked.

"I heard it starts when kids turn ten," I said. "It's to do with maturity."

It also happens when you have to buy a marzipan.

"How come you're home, Mr. Melon?" Sam asked.

"I'm taking my lovely wife to Montmartre for lunch," he said. "Then I'm going to the office for a big meeting."

"I've never been to a meeting," Sam said. "Are they exciting?"

My dad laughed. "I'll tell the Congressman you asked."

"Thanks," Sam said.

My mother came out wearing a striped dress and red high heels. She goes insane over restaurants. I think it's because they don't serve diet yogurt.

"I'm anxious to try this place," my mom said.

"Me too," my dad said. "I've been daydreaming about frog legs for a week."

"Why?" Sam asked.

"They're the chef's special dish," my dad said. "Sautéed in butter, garlic, and French herbs."

"To eat?" I yelled. "You're going to eat a frog's legs?"

My dad nodded.

"How is the frog supposed to get around without legs?" Sam said.

"You could be eating somebody's pet," I said. "Did you ever think of that?"

"Sorry, Sport," my dad said. "But J. A. Fischer said, 'The frog legs are a must-eat!' So I must eat."

"That's peer pressure," I said. "What if I did everything Bart Bigelow told me to do?"

"You'd be a major cusser who farts on purpose," Sam said.

"I forbid you to be a Bigelow," my mom said.

I wanted to say, "I forbid Dad to eat an innocent frog's legs," but that's the kind of remark my parents call going too far.

"I hope they taste disgusting," I said.

"J. A. Fischer is never wrong," my dad said.

"Except when he attacked Chez François's creamed onions," my mom said.

"I'm in favor of attacking onions," I said.

My parents laughed.

"Are you also eating defenseless amphibian legs?" I asked my mom.

"I'm ordering bouillabaisse," she said.

"What's that?" Sam asked.

"Fish stew," my mom said.

"What have you people got against sea creatures?" I asked.

"It's a 'creamy, dreamy medley, with undercurrents of ocean spray,' according to Mr. Fischer and the *Food Revue*," she said.

"I've never eaten medley," I said.

"Or undercurrents," Sam said. "Whatever they are."

"Currants are the same as raisins," I told him.

My dad roughed up my hair with his hand. "Behave yourself, Sport. I can't keep a pretty lady waiting."

"Are you talking about Mrs. Melon?" Sam asked.

My mom hung on my dad's elbow. Otherwise her high heels get stuck between the sidewalk bricks. High heels are another lady habit I don't get.

They got to Goodneighbor Dave's before my mom turned back and yelled, "No prank-calling your grandmother."

"I know that now," I said.

"Get the periscope," Sam said. "My butt can't survive another day in the tree."

12

UNDERCOVER UNDER CARDBOARD

Sam and I built our periscope last year when we were in fourth grade. It's made of plastic pipes and mirrors. If you were in a submarine you could look through the bottom pipe and see what was happening on top of the ocean. It also works on land. Hide behind a tree or in a bush. It is unnoticeable to people with average eyes.

"Ready, Eddie?" Sam said.

"Follow me, Flea. I'll take the light off my bike. You can sit on the handlebars and carry the scope."

For the whole ride Sam talked like he was rich. When we got to Eastern Market he said, "Thank you, Driver. Very good pedaling."

Mrs. Calamaris was arranging pomegranates at her fruit and vegetable stand.

"May we have your two hugest boxes?" I asked.

"Hokey-dokey," she said.

"We're on the trail of a lady criminal," I whispered.

I could not believe I blurted it out.

Mrs. Calamaris laughed. "Big stuff! What did this lady criminal do?"

"Menace society," I said.

She pinched my cheek like I was a baby.

Mrs. Calamaris came to America from Greece and learned English when she got here. I don't think she knows *menace* yet. It's not a funny word.

"Unpack the bananas and red onions," she said. "Those are my biggest boxes."

"Double luck!" I said. "I always wanted to be a fruit unloader."

"Anytime," she said.

"Can I borrow your box cutter?" Sam asked.

"No," she said.

"We need eyeholes," Sam said.

"I'll cut one hole on each box. That's all. I have kiwis to arrange," she said.

"How about a slot?" I asked.

"What do you mean, a slot?" she asked.

"A slit," I said. "The size of your red pencil."

"Right here?" she asked.

"If there's ever a contest for fastest cutting, sign up. You'll win," Sam said.

"Mrs. Calamaris," I whispered. "I was joking when I said that about the lady menace."

"I know that," she said.

Sam picked up his box and asked, "Where can we buy a marzipan?"

"Try Hill's Kitchen," Mrs. Calamaris said.

We walked about ten steps out of Eastern Market and crashed dead into Pop.

"Sorry," I said. "It's impossible to see over this box."

"It was unavoidable, then," Pop said. "Why the boxes?"

"We're going to sit under them," Sam said.

"Sounds like an excellent way to spend an afternoon," Pop said.

"I hope so," I said.

"Do you need any help at your house?" Sam asked him. "We're for hire."

"I was just thinking that I shouldn't build a gazebo by myself," Pop said.

"If I had money I'd pay you for that job," I said.

"You get us for half price if you pay today," Sam said.

"It's the Sizzling Summer Steal of a Deal," I said. I'm a fast thinker with a talent for slogans.

"I am keen on deals," Pop said. "Do you think ten dollars is fair?"

"Ultra," I said. "But we can't start until we finish a project."

Pop looked in his wallet. "Will fives do?"

"Do what?" Sam asked.

"Do for now," Pop said.

Sam and I sat on the Divas' brick wall and untied our high-tops.

I pushed my bill into the toe of my shoe. Sam likes to lay his flat so it's under his whole foot.

"I see why it's called walking-around money," Pop said.

"It's the portable bank of Converse," I said. "Get it?"

"I do," Pop said. "I'm naturally quick-witted."

"Don't put change in the Bank of C," Sam said. "Unless you're wishing for blisters."

"Good tip," Pop said. "But I need my money handy. I'm on the way to buy Madam an anniversary present."

"Get a ham," I said. "My mom says everybody likes a ham."

"First-rate idea," Pop said. "I have never given Madam pork."

"See you tonight," Sam said.

"For the cake-making extravaganza," Pop said. "A big time will be had."

"My bike will be safe in the Divas' patio," I told Sam.

Jonique was swinging on the gate.

"What's up?" Sam asked.

"Math camp in an hour," she said. "What's up with the boxes?"

"No offense," I said. "But it's private and confidential."

"I am a great secret keeper," she said.

"This is a government secret," Sam said.

"I might know it already," Jonique said. "But I wouldn't tell you if I did because it's a secret."

"You don't know it," I said.

"If you say so," she said.

"We do," Sam said. "It's impossible."

Jonique smiled. Then she shrugged.

"If you know it, give us a hint," I said.

"I don't give hints," she said.

"Is it about a criminal?" Sam asked.

"It would be irresponsible for me to tell you," she said.

"Does your secret involve the FBI?" I asked.

She pretended to zip her lips.

"All right," I said. "We'll tell you a little. Then you tell us if we have the same secret."

After we finished, all Jonique could say was "I am shocked to my bones" and "Are you positive?"

"The FBI doesn't make mistakes," I said.

"Then you're crazy!" she said. "Being Junior Agents doesn't mean you should chase after a Most Wanted by yourselves."

"Junior *Special* Agents," I said.

"All we're doing is finding evidence," Sam said.

"I bet you didn't tell your parents," Jonique said.

"Mrs. Wilkins thinks we should do it," I said.

"Well, she is a good judge of danger," Jonique said. "Just don't be a Melonhead, Melonhead."

13

JUNIOR SPECIAL AGENTS BTG

Sam and I crept down the walking alley.

"Stay close to the wall," I told him.

He checked by periscope. "No Chameleon in sight."

We went over the plan.

1. Crawl by parked cars.

2. Stop near the fire hydrant that's near the pin oak.

3. Pull the box over your body.

4. Sit and wait.

"Juice boxes?" Sam asked.

"Check."

"Fruit Roll-Ups?

"Check."

"Cereal?"

"Check."

"Whistle?"

"Check," I said. "Camera?"

"Check," Sam said.

"You lead," I told him.

We ran as fast as anybody can run when they're bent in half and dragging boxes.

"Halt!" Sam whispered. "Two people. Coming this way. One could be the Chameleon."

"No way," I whispered back. "That lady's wider."

We ducked behind a city trash can.

"Are you positive?" Sam asked. "Because they're about fifteen seconds away from us!"

"Stop! Drop! Box!" I said.

I drop-sat, threw my head down, and pulled my knees up so fast I smashed myself in my eye sockets. For a second I thought I'd knocked my eyeballs out. Then I realized I was in the dark because Sam had thrown my box over me. It smelled like onions.

"Are you undercover?" I whispered.

"Yeah," Sam said. "Can't you see me?"

"My eye slot is on the wrong side," I said. "I'm packed too tight to turn."

"Quiet," Sam whispered.

I pretended I was a frozen mastodon. A frozen mastodon who was sitting like a frog.

If people could've seen how much I was sweating, they'd have thought I was crying. I was not.

Grumpy lady's voice.

"Why do people leave trash in the tree box? The recycle can is right there."

The Chameleon! She must have jaywalked across the street.

THIS SIDE UP

Even though I had brain shock, I made a silent promise: Whoever the litterer is, I am their friend for infinity. The trash distraction was pure luck.

"They're just cardboard boxes," the man said. "I'll throw them away."

Boxes?

My heart stopped. It started right back up, going a thousand beats a minute. The thump on top of my box made it go even faster. In my mind I could see through it like it was glass. I could picture the accomplice. He had hairy arms and giant hands. They were about to pull off my hideout. A light sliver came through the slot. My head felt weak.

I heard a creak.

"The can's pretty full," the lady said. "But they'll fit if you crush them."

Oh, my sweet potato. I am doomed.

I could probably have poked the Chameleon in the knee with a stick through my eye slot.

Not that I would. It would be insane to provoke an MW.

"You're the boss," the man said.

Proof. But I won't live to tell the FBI.

"Stop," the Chameleon said. "They could be the Andersons'. They're auction hounds."

What are action hounds? Ack. Attack dogs. I'm doomed times infinity.

The Chameleon kept talking. "Sometimes the Andersons unload on the sidewalk and rush off to park before traffic piles up."

They just leave attack dogs on the sidewalk?

"I don't want them to come back and find us holding their figurines," the Chameleon said.

"Figurines?" the man asked.

What about the hounds? I am begging you! Go away! Leave now. Scram.

"Their house is a regular figurine museum," the Chameleon said. "They have a fortune invested in tiny statues. Animals. Children. Children with animals. Elves. Gnomes. Fairies. Hundreds of them. Ceramics for every occasion."

She let out an evil laugh.

My heart was banging so hard it felt like it was bruising my kidneys. Or lungs. Or whatever valuable organs are next to hearts.

It's a terrible feeling to know you're a second from death.

Walk away from the boxes.

They laughed like the criminals they are.

Then came the sound of slapping.

Save Sam.

I hugged my wobbly knees to keep them from jiggling my box.

Stand up! Defend Sam!

I couldn't move.

Sam's getting pulverized while I'm planning my plan!

I am a wuss. Worse than a wuss. I have a chicken heart.

Save your friend.

There was a battle of confusion in my head. The smacks were getting lighter.

What if they knocked him out with drops? What if they're carrying him away right now?

14

BUTT-WALKING TO SAFETY

In the background I could hear city noises. They were soft, drowned out by my breathing. I sounded like my mom. She has zero bravery.

I heard a hiss. "Melonhead."

Sam!

Supersonic brain-to-brain message: *QUIET! YOU'LL GIVE US AWAY!*

He didn't receive it.

"They're gone," Sam said.

My Fear flew out.

"They went in the Chameleon's house."

I whispered, "Are you hurt?"

"Why would I be?"

"I heard her slapping you," I said.

"Slapping?" Sam asked.

"You don't have to fake courage around me."

"I'm not," Sam said. "I'm terrified to my inner bones. But they didn't hit me."

"I heard smacking," I said.

"Flip-flops," he said. "When they were walking away. We got safer with every flip."

"Sorry you had to do all the spying," I said.

"Not all. Sometimes I was too scared to look," he said. "But I took a picture through my eye slot."

"That's professional FBI thinking!" I said. "Is it safe to spin my box around?"

"Carefully," Sam said. "All our protection drove away. It's rush hour."

If you don't move your car before rush hour a police tow truck takes it away.

By the time I could see out of my eye slot, I had a plan. "We'll crawl like slugs," I said. "Slugs wearing boxes."

"Smart," Sam said. "If we go slow nobody will notice the boxes are moving."

Crawling in a box is not as easy as you'd think. Your feet take a two-inch step to the edge of the box. Your leg muscles drag your butt forward. Or, if you're me, backward. That's so we had double vision. Nobody could sneak up on us this time.

"We'll be teenagers by the time we get home," Sam said.

"At least this is a cement sidewalk," I said. "If we were on my block we'd be butt-walking on brick. The corners would stab us."

"Think of a signal for 'Someone is coming,'" Sam said.

"A toucan squawk," I said.

"What do toucans sound like?" Sam asked.

"RRRRK, RRRRK," I said.

"My shirt's soaking wet from sweat," he said.

"Ditto," I said.

"I want out," Sam said.

"Keep going," I said. "If we de-box where people can see, the Chameleon might hear about it. Once we turn the corner and make it to Tom Harrison's, we're free."

"We'll duck behind their mini-lions," Sam said.

"I told my mom we should get cement lions if she wants to win the next garden contest. She refused."

"Friction from the sidewalk is giving me a hot butt," Sam said.

I laughed so hard Sam thought I was doing the toucan squawk.

"It's a good thing we can't go fast," I said. "That much friction could start a butt fire."

Sam's laugh came out in a snort. "I sound like Pop," he said.

I toucanned. "RRRRK! RRRRK!"

"Very funny," Sam said.

"Lady alert," I said. "RRRRK!"

She was a slow one.

"How far to the bend?" I asked after she passed.

"I'd say twelve feet."

All I wanted was to leap up and run for it.

"RRRRK," Sam squawked. "Man with stroller."

The guy was so close that all I could see through

my eye slot was tan cloth and a hairy knee. I heard sniffing noises. My mom says that happens when people don't put hats on babies.

"Come on, Veronica," the man said. "Do your business."

I almost laughed out loud. What kind of business can a baby have? Also, who ever heard of a baby named Veronica?

My box rocked. I pressed my hands against the inside walls. My eye slot was blocked so I was in the dark again. In my brain I heard Agent Atkin. *A good investigator uses all the senses.*

I put my finger through the slot and touched gently with my index finger. Hair. Unhatted baby head.

Get going, people. And stop scratching my box, mister.

Light was coming in from the bottom. A puddle. I must have sat on my juice box.

"Good girl, Veronica," the man said.

"Oggie bee," the baby said.

Thanks to Julia I understand baby language. I wished I didn't.

When they were too far away to hear, I yell-whispered to Sam. "You said MAN! You said STROLLER! You NEVER said DOG!"

"I didn't have time," Sam said.

"My box is soggy," I said.

"Scoot along," Sam said.

"Quit laughing," I said.

"I can't help it," Sam said. "Being peed on by a dog is funny."

"My box got peed on," I said. "Not me. FBI agents get in gross situations every day."

"You'd laugh if it happened to me," Sam said.

"True."

"I have never been this happy to turn a corner," Sam said.

"Ditto," I said. "My butt hurts."

"Can't we crawl from here?" Sam asked.

"Our feet will stick out," I said.

"I don't care," Sam said.

"I've got cricket legs. They're permanently bent."

"Is your coast clear?" I asked.

"Totally," he said.

"Mine too," I said.

"My legs thank you," Sam said.

"Mine don't. The sidewalk is scalding."

We made two yards of progress. Then Sam said, "Crawling is actually worse than butt-walking. The sidewalk feels like number ten sandpaper."

Pop says that's the roughest number there is.

"Going backward makes me carsick."

Finally Sam yelled. "Halleluia! I'm head-butting the Harrisons' gate. Head for the lions."

Their walkway feels a lot longer when you do it on your knees.

I punched the ceiling of my box. It flipped over the lion, into the yard.

"My muscles are spazzing," Sam said.

I started to say, "Double for me." Instead I said, "There's blood on the Harrisons' flagstone!"

"Fresh blood!" Sam said. "Smeared fresh blood."

"The Chameleon struck!" I said.

"Save the Harrisons!" Sam said.

We beat our fists on their double doors.

Finally one opened.

"Mrs. Harrison!" I screamed. "You're alive."

"Why, yes, I am," she said.

"Then whose blood is on your walk?" I asked.

She looked over our heads. She stared down at Sam and me.

"Yours?" she asked.

Creeks of blood were rolling out of all four of our knees and into our shoes. "They're mini-scrapes," I  said. "I get them all the time. There's no reason to call my mom."

"None at all," Sam said.

"That's a lot of mini-scrapes," Mrs. Harrison said. "I'll send Tom out with Band-Aids. You guys hose down my walkway before rumors start."

"We'll need a lot of soap," Sam said.

"No, you won't," Mrs. Harrison said. "Water will do the job. And get those boxes out of the yard."

"We're happy to help," I said.

She smiled. "You might give yourselves a splash. Something out here smells dreadful."

"Like onions mixed with dog pee," I said.

"How do you come up with such horrifying ideas?" Mrs. Harrison asked.

Sam and I soaked our heads under the spigot. I blasted Sam. It's too bad Tom came out that second. He never minds being wet, but his mom is particular about the hall.

"Sorry," I yelled. "I didn't expect the door to open."

"It's okay," Tom said. "If we mop up fast my mom will never know the floor got wet."

I dried the mail on the back of Tom's shirt. Tom swabbed the floor with his brother's karate jacket.

"The only Band-Aids we have are the useless dots," he said.

"They're for girls," Sam said.

"We don't need any," I said.

"You're already getting scabs," Tom said.

Sam tied his shirt around his head.

We walked the long way around to get my bike. Sam drove. I directed from the handlebars. We stopped at the S.E. Library. Luckily they have a garden with a water fountain. Stakeouts are double dehydrators.

"Let's sit on the dirt and look at the photos," Sam said.

"Your mom was smart to buy a waterproof camera," I said. "Otherwise we'd be burnt toast."

"The first picture is the figurine museum," Sam said.

"It looks like a house," I said.

"The Frederick Douglass Museum looks like a house," Sam said.

"That's because he used to live in it," I said.

"Maybe the figurine people live in their museum."

He clicked to the next picture.

"Wrong lady," I said. "Her butt's too big. It's a grandmother butt."

"You're an expert on grandmother butts?" Sam said.

"This is not the butt of the Chameleon," I said.

"This is the lady who was talking about the figurine museum," Sam said.

"What's on her head?"

"The tallest, reddest wig ever made," Sam said.

"Next time aim the camera at her face," I said.

Sam wrote in the Log.

Talks like Chameleon. Has elderly walk. Flowered pants (baggy), blue shirt (loose), yellow pocketbook. Flip-flops. Black high heels in hand. Picture is Chameleon.

I wrote in the Log.

Picture is not Chameleon.

"Ready to ride, Clyde?" I asked.

"Did you just hear somebody say 'Yo! Melonhead!'?" Sam said.

"It's Justin!" I said. "He's over there."

Justin is our best teenager friend.

"Hi, Justin!" I waved my arms like a person on a desert island who wants to be rescued.

"Melonhead, you're a mess," he said.

"Thanks," I told him. "You are too."

"So am I!" Sam yelled.

"Got to roll," Justin said.

"We're rolling to Hill's Kitchen," Sam said.

I locked my bike to the Kitchen fence.

The first thing the store owner said was "You may leave your helmets and the pipes by the door."

"It's a periscope," Sam said.

The second thing was "You're Melonhead, aren't you?"

"Yes, ma'am," I said. "This is Sam."

"I've heard of you," she said.

"Lots of people tell us that," I said.

Her name tag said Leah.

"We need to buy a marzipan," Sam said.

She smiled. "What's it for?"

"To cook in," Sam said.

I think if you are the boss of a cooking store you should know that.

We walked past the garlic squeezers and bottle stoppers shaped like pigs. Sam bumped into the cookie cutter rack. That made me knock over some rolling pins. Ms. Leah handed me a small log. It was wrapped in gold paper that said Almond Paste.

"No offense," I said. "But we don't need nut paste." Who would?

"We need a PAN," Sam explained.

"Marzipan is almond," she said. "It's delicious."

"It's for cakes?" Sam asked.

She nodded. "It works like Play-Doh. You can make cake decorations out of it."

"Sold," I said.

Sam and I took off our shoes and pulled out our Pop money and our weeding fee.

"It's wet from sweat," I said.

"I can feel," Ms. Leah said.

Sam and I ate the rest of my Shredded Wheat to make pocket room for the marzipan.

"No wonder the Divas charge a lot," I said. "You could go broke buying marzipan."

15
I FEEL A BREEZE

My mom saw us from a block away.

"Lucky we're walking your bike," Sam said. My mom thinks riding on the handlebars is a top danger.

"Why does she have a stormy look?" I said.

My mom's high heels click-clacked down the sidewalk.

"Mrs. Bruce called. Mr. Gold emailed," she yelled.

"What did we do?" Sam whispered.

"No clue," I said.

She was getting closer.

"Her lips look mad," Sam said.

Her voice sounded madder. "I let you do something once, you make it an everyday thing."

Mrs. Lee was watching us from her porch. "What is he doing every day?" she yelled.

Mrs. Lee turns up whenever somebody is embarrassed or in trouble. My mom ignored her.

"What is so amusing about wandering around the neighborhood making people think you're injured?" she said.

"I don't know," I said. "What?"

"Adam, ketchup is not a toy!" she said. "It's a food. And it stains."

"I know," I said.

She was speed-stomping. Then her legs froze. Her body kept going. She wiggled and jerked.

"Stay balanced and hold on," I yelled. "We're coming."

"My heel's stuck between bricks," she said.

Mrs. Lee ran down her steps. "I will be the one to help," she told my mom. "They are not good boys."

Even when my mom has had it with me, she does not like Mrs. Lee making accusations.

"They ARE good boys," my mom snapped. "Great boys. The best boys."

"Lean on me, Mom," I said.

"They are bad," Mrs. Lee said. "They gave my dog a haircut with no permission."

"It's easy to get small, fluffy dogs mixed up," my mom said.

"Not Pinky," Mrs. Lee said. "She is a show dog."

"Pinky was in the Rosens' yard," my mom said. "And the Rosens wanted their dog's hair cut."

"By children?" Mrs. Lee asked.

"That was a misunderstanding," my mom said.

I squatted. "Mom, I'm pulling your leg," I said. "Not pulling your leg like I'm joking. I'm actually pulling it."

"I can feel that, Adam," my mom said.

"Don't panic, Mrs. Melon," Sam told her. "I've got your other leg in a death grip."

I yanked with all my might.

"Unbuckle the strap," my mother said.

"I know what I'm doing, Mom," I said. "G for

L number eight. I'm Remembering the Ways of Ladies. And I know about being stuck."

"In trees," Mrs. Lee said.

"Once," my mom said. "One time he was stuck in a tree."

"Pull forward," Sam said.

"Heave ho!" I yelled.

I might have over-pulled. My mom kicked me in the shoulder on her way to sitting on Sam.

"Owww," Sam said. "You weigh a ton, Mrs. Melon."

"Great news," I said. "Your foot is free!"

"People will think you're giving your mom's foot away," Sam said.

"And my new sandal survived," my mom said.

"Not so!" Mrs. Lee said. "It is ruined."

The red straps and the sole were on my mom's foot. The heel was still in the crack.

I gave it a tug. "Did you see that, Mom?" I said. "It popped out like it was buttered. How lucky is that?"

"It's hard to believe my luck," she said.

"We can nail that heel back on in a hot second," Sam said.

"Or staple it," I said. "Your choice."

"I'm hoisting you up by your armpits," Sam said.

"I do not need hoisting," my mom said. "I am capable."

"I don't mind," Sam said.

"Blood!" Mrs. Lee said. "It's on your dress."

"It's ketchup," my mom said.

"Not ketchup," Mrs. Lee said. "Blood."

"Ketchup," my mom said. "Thank goodness. Bloodstains are impossible."

"It's not your blood," Sam said. "It's ours."

"I just noticed our knees are spouting again," I said.

Sam looked. "More of a flow, I'd say."

"Who hurt you?" my mom asked.

"Nobody," I said.

"Were you on the roof again?" she asked.

"The roof?" Mrs. Lee said. "That is very bad."

My mom gave Mrs. Lee her sharpest look and said, "We are leaving now."

I would have enjoyed it more if my mom hadn't been dragging Sam and me by our wrists.

"You know what would be funny, Mom? If you were pulling Dad's suitcase. Busted heel, busted wheel. You're both lopsided."

She did not laugh.

"I see your skivvies," Mrs. Lee said.

"What are skivvies?" Sam asked.

"Underwear," my mom said.

Then she let go and stepped back.

"Put your hands on your bottoms and run inside."

"Why?" I said at the same time my palms landed.

I took off like lightning. Sam was lightning sprayed with WD-40.

My mom shut the door fast.

"How did you get holes on the back of your pants?" she said. "It was the Normans' dog, wasn't it? I always said it's dangerous for dogs the size of cows to live in a city with children."

"It wasn't a dog," Sam said.

"I guess it happened when we were butt-walking on the sidewalk," I said.

"Your pockets are gone," Sam said.

"More than your pockets," my mom said.

"I see London," Sam sang.

I ran behind him. "I see France," I said.

"You're lucky it's only your underpants that are on display," my mom said. "Didn't you feel the seat of your shorts disappearing?"

"Not at all," Sam said.

"We were going slow," I said.

"Ms. Leah saw our underwear!" Sam said. "Justin, too."

I could feel my face heating up. "I've got childhood drama," I said.

"That's childhood trauma," my mom said. "And you don't have it. You're just embarrassed."

"We'll go sit in the basement," I said.

That's where I get sent whenever I'm a danger to furniture.

"Get two pairs of clean underwear and two pairs of clean shorts from the laundry room," she said. "After you change, sit on the plastic chairs. I'll be down with the first-aid kit."

First we got scrubbed with soapy water.

"What could be more germ-filled than a sidewalk?" she asked.

I guessed. "An ape's mouth?"

"A toilet," Sam said.

"An ape's mouth after it drinks out of the toilet," I said.

Hydrogen peroxide is my favorite first aid. When it hits a cut, it fizzes white bubbles. After we got a layer of Neosporin and Band-Aids, my mom called Sam's dad. Her report made it sound like our legs were falling off.

16
A CLUE

"I'm home," my dad yelled.

"Thank goodness!" my mom said.

"It feels good to be missed," he said.

"This has been a ninety-hour day," my mom said. "Except for lunch, which wasn't long enough."

"What happened?" he asked.

"Ask the boy who came home with his behind barely covered and his legs striped with blood," she said. "It's unbelievable."

"Sam and I were butt-walking," I said. "Then we crawled on the sidewalk."

"I believe that," my dad said.

"Why would ten-year-old boys crawl like babies?" my mom asked.

"It's a boy thing, Betty," my dad said.

"It's goofy," she said.

"Yes, it is," my dad said.

My mom pointed at her G for L poster. She used a load of alien stickers. She thinks they make me pay attention.

She pointed. "Number one."

"I'm more shocked than anybody, Mom," I said. "It's amazing that butt-walking was the Cause of that Effect."

My dad got up to answer the phone. When he came back he said, "That was Sam's mom."

"Was she blaming Adam for Sam's knees?" my mom said. "Because it was Sam's idea too."

"She didn't mention knees," my dad said. "She wanted us to know that our son was a huge help this morning."

"Really?" my mom said.

"The boys took care of Julia," my dad told her.

"Mrs. Alswang wanted to unclog the toilet in peace," I said.

My dad laughed.

"It was Legos this time," I said.

"How did that sweet little girl get so interested in flushing?" my mom asked.

I did not care to answer that.

"Plus she dumped in a bottle of baby shampoo," I said. "But the big trouble was Mrs. Alswang's wrinkle cream. The jar got stuck. It wouldn't go up and it wouldn't go down."

"I think it's marvelous that Mrs. Alswang does her own plumbing," my mom said.

"She says it's too expensive to have a live-in plumber," I said.

"Well, she has a tip-top babysitter in my Darling Boy," my mom said.

"How did you keep Julia amused?" my dad asked.

"We played Spin the Baby," I said. "Then I let her pick my nose."

"Oh, dear," my mom said.

"I said, 'Julia, that's my nose.' She said, 'Manos,' and poked her spare index finger in my other nostril. She has sharp nails for a baby."

"Babies should not play in noses," my mom said. "Did you Hanitizer her?"

Out of all my inventions, the germ-killing lotion is my mom's favorite.

"No."

"Sam said, 'Julia, you can pick your friends and you can pick your nose, but you can't pick your friend's nose.'"

"That's too complicated for a baby to understand," my mom said.

"She's smart," I said. "She learned to say 'picnose.'"

"Why would you teach a little girl such an unpleasant word?" my mom said.

"She taught it to us," I said.

We had quiche for dinner. It tastes like cheese pie. I was on my third piece when a picture of the Chameleon's butt flashed in my mind.

"Mom," I said. "Do you know

how sometimes you say 'These pants make me look fat'?"

"Sport," my dad said. "That is not a question ladies enjoy."

"I'm asking for a reason," I said. "Do stores sell fattening pants?"

"Yes," my mom said. "But they don't call them that."

"What do they call them?" I asked.

"Seventy percent off."

"Strange name," I said.

My dad thought it was hilarious.

After dinner I called Sam and told him the news.

"Fattening pants are *behind* the Chameleon's big butt?" Sam said.

"I can't believe I didn't figure out all those ladies were the same person," I said.

"I knew I had the right lady," he said.

"See you soon, Calhoon," I said.

"Be ready to bake, Jake."

17
MAKING IT RIGHT

My dad walked Sam and me to Madam and Pop's.

"Sam's dad will pick up the boys," he told Pop. "Thanks for inviting them over."

Madam and Pop have the top kitchen on Capitol Hill.

"Pop, remember when I was in third grade I could fit inside the dumbwaiter?"

"It's a comfort to know you've outgrown it," Pop said.

"Not to me," I said.

"Let's get baking," Sam said.

"Madam left the recipe and the ingredients on the counter," Pop said. "The mixer, bowls, and cake pans are on the table. And your sous-chef is standing next to you."

"What's *soo?*" Sam asked.

"It means I do what you say."

"Whatever we tell you, no matter what?" I said.

"I won't dance like a monkey," Pop said.

That made me hoot like one.

"Actually, I enjoy dancing like a monkey," he said. "But sous-chefs are helpers. They do the less interesting jobs. If there is a lull, sous-chefs can work on a crossword puzzle."

"I like being the boss," I said.

"I'll be the boss's boss," Sam said.

"You know what?" I said. "Cake making uses all the G for Ls."

"Except for Honesty Is the Only Policy," Sam said.

"And I'm hoping you can avoid

If You Do Something Wrong, Make It Right," Pop said.

I was going to say, "That G for L is why we're making the cake." But Sam interrupted, "The name of the cake is Foolproof."

"First Instruction. 'Turn the oven to three hundred and fifty degrees,'" I read.

Pop showed us how. I turned it off and back on.

"I always wanted to do that," I told him.

"Back up, Gumbo," Sam said. "An oven is no place for a poodle. Too hot."

"I'll turn up the ceiling fan," I said.

"It says put in one teaspoon of baking soda," Sam said.

"Madam keeps the ginger ale in the washstand," I said.

"I never heard of cooking soda pop," Sam said. "It sounds crazy."

"You want to hear crazy?" I said. "My mom makes biscuit dough with milk."

"Baking soda is in that orange box on the counter," Pop said. "It makes cakes rise. And we'll need baking powder, too."

"That was a close one," I said.

"Mix in two cups all-purpose flour," Sam said.

"What other purpose does flour have?" I asked.

"I once used flour to make a fine pair of bedroom slippers," Pop said. "Huge success."

"How did you make them?" Sam asked.

"I got my feet wet and dipped them in the bag of flour," he said.

"Can we do it now?" I asked.

"It's too late," Pop said. "Without sunshine they'll never dry. And they're no good wet. They stick to the floor."

"Are you joking?" I asked.

"Yes," he said.

"I knew it," I said.

"But you should have seen the cornmeal gloves I made for Madam."

That got us laughing like nuts. The laughing made Gumbo jump around the table. The shock of a wet nose on Sam's elbow made him drop the flour. Which turned Gumbo's black curls gray. That made her run back and forth in a panic, which made puffs of flour fly off of her coat. I blame the fan for spreading it around the kitchen floor.

"Come on, Gumbo," Pop said. "Let's shake it off in the yard."

"I'll clean the floor," I said. "Sam can keep cooking."

"I'm trading in one and one-third cups of sugar for honey," Sam said. "Because that's all we have. The rest spilled on the book. Pages are sticking."

"Peel them apart," I said.

"I did. Words tore off."

"That's okay," I told him. "Everything you need is on the counter."

It turns out flour really sticks to brick-tile floors.

"Toss me a wet sponge," I said.

"Is a spoon and a half of allspice enough?" Sam asked.

"I'd say so," I told him.

"I can read the cinnamon," he said. "It's one teaspoon. What are cloves?"

"Garlic," I said, and passed him a clear bag of brown powder. "This must be it."

"The cloves are called ground," Sam said.

"Probably because it looks like dirt," I said.

Sam put the can under my nose.

"It doesn't smell like garlic," I said.

"Should I use it?" Sam asked.

"Just a pinch of it," I said. "And don't turn the mixer on high."

"I'll never do that again," he said.

I looked at the counter. "All that's left is butter, two eggs, and tomato soup," I said.

"I never heard of soup in a cake," Sam said.

"I never heard of garlic," I said. "But it seems okay."

Sam unwrapped the butter and cracked the eggs. I opened the can.

To be extra careful, we dialed the mixer knob to four.

"Should it be this thick?" Sam asked.

I poured in some water and Sam remixed. We tested by licking the beaters.

"Better batter," Sam said.

"Tastes good," I said. Then I stopped. My mom somehow got the idea that eating raw eggs is bad for you.

The back door opened. "We're back," Pop said. "And Gumbo is only lightly floured."

"So are the pans," Sam said. "But they're supposed to be dusted."

"How's the floor?" Pop said.

"When you said flour slippers stick to floors, I thought that was part of the joke," I said.

"You washed the flour?" Pop asked.

"And it turned to paste," I said. "I could not have been more shocked."

Sam rubbed the pans with the butter wrapper. Pop poured the batter. There was enough left for a cupcake. By the time the dinger went off, Sam and I had scraped the paste off the floor.

"We're sorry for the mess," Sam said.

"And the dog," I said. "And the book, of course."

"And getting honey on your crosswords."

"Do you wish you went to the neighborhood meeting instead of helping us?" I asked.

"I would rather scrape the floor with my toenails than go to that meeting," Pop said.

"And I did learn from the experience," I told him.

"You have learned an extraordinary amount for a boy your age," Pop said.

"Thanks," I said.

"Let's have a glass of milk," Pop said. "By the time we think of an eight-letter word for *lazy*, the cakes will be cool."

"We can't think," Sam said. "We have marzipan flowers to make."

I opened the package from Hill's Kitchen.

"Is all marzipan white?" I asked.

"We need the pink and light green kind," Sam said.

Pop pinched off a piece and squished it in his fingers. "What you need is food coloring," he said. "Fortunately, Madam seems to have stockpiled several colors."

He gave me a bottle of green. Sam got red.

"Use a wee amount," Pop said.

"Thank you," I said.

I broke the marzipan log. Sam karate-chopped his.

"I'm starting with four drops," Sam said.

"Ditto," I said.

"Work it like dough," Pop said.

"My pink is turning red," I said.

"Mine is overly green," Sam said.

"Pop?" I said. "How do we fix it?"

"Red roses will look fine," Pop said.

"They have to look the same," I said.

"The same as what?" Pop asked.

"The Divas'," I said.

That led to the story of the tree.

We left the Chameleon out of it. I don't know why. Pop is all for capturing criminals.

"So this is a replacement cake," Pop said.

"That's the perfect word for it," I said.

"My leaves look good," Sam said.

"Is Mrs. Bazoo paying for this cake?" Pop asked.

"We're not getting the money," I said. "She's paying Mrs. McBee."

"And Mrs. Bazoo thinks her cake is being made by Divas," Pop said.

"Right. Mrs. McBee gets money. Mrs. Bazoo's sister gets her cake," I said. "It's the same as if the cake never fell out of the tree."

Sam nodded. "No harm. No foul."

"Have you thought about telling Mrs. McBee what happened?" Pop asked.

"No," I said. "She could fire us."

"That's true," Pop said.

"Otherwise we would," I said.

"It would take courage," Pop said.

That made me think about when I thought Sam was getting slapped.

"Do you think I don't have any?" I asked.

"You have plenty," he said. "You'll figure it out."

Whatever that means.

"You know what?" I said. "If my mom could see this cake, she'd say I could do all the cooking every day."

"You could show her," Pop said.

"It's a private cake," Sam said.

"You can't see the hole," I said. "Thanks to the marzipan roses."

"They distract from the slope," Sam said.

"The slope that adds to the cake's look," I said. "It's kind of, what's the word?"

"Jaunty?" Pop said.

"Right," Sam said. "It's a jaunty cake."

"What do you call a boy diva?" I asked.

"A devo?" Sam said.

"We're the Baking Devos," I said.

The first thing Mr. Alswang asked was "What's under the tinfoil?"

"I'd rather not say," I told him.

He looked at the little foil tent in Sam's green hands.

"It's the same thing, only smaller," Sam said.

Since I couldn't wave, I yelled. "Good night, Pop. Thanks!"

"Good night, boys," Pop said.

"Sleep well," Sam's dad told Pop.

"He's waiting up for Madam to get home. She's at the neighborhood meeting," Sam said.

"Week three of the Great Park Bench Debate," Mr. Alswang said. "Madam's a good citizen."

"I'd rather poke myself with a stick than sit in a folding chair and listen to Fred Neenobber's presentation on bench safety," Pop said. "Thankfully, I had guests tonight so I didn't have to do either."

Mr. Alswang laughed. "She'll be gone another two hours at least."

"I told her to make a night of it," Pop said. "I've got a book about President Eisenhower to read and a nice can of tomato soup for a midnight snack."

I almost dropped Mrs. Bazoo's cake.

"Dad," Sam said. "Can we stop at Mrs. Wilkins's on the way home?"

"If her downstairs lights are on, you can run in for a minute," Mr. Alswang said.

Molly opened the door. "It's late," she said. "I'm about to fix Mom an egg."

Why, I do not know. Nobody feels better from eating an egg.

"Don't just stand there," Mrs. Wilkins yelled.

We ran around Molly. "We made you a mini-cake," I said. "It's still hot."

"Smells like Paris," Mrs. Wilkins said.

"Is that a good thing?" Sam asked.

"It's a great thing," she said.

I waited for her to say something snappish but she didn't.

"Mrs. Wilkins," I said. "What would you do if you wanted to follow somebody but you didn't want them to see you?"

"I'd just follow them," she said. "Nobody notices old ladies."

"I do," I said. "They're all over the place."

"Probably why I like you better than I like most people," she said.

"You do?"

"Don't get big-headed," she said. "I don't like a lot of people."

Molly came back with scrambled eggs, pills, and whole-wheat toast.

"I'm eating dessert first," Mrs. Wilkins said. "It's not big enough to share."

"Really, Mom," Molly said. "What kind of grown-up are you?"

18

A BRILLIANT IDEA

I got to Sam's so early his parents were still asleep.

"Yo! Joe," Sam said.

"Bewenhid," Julia said. She doesn't get rhyming.

I put her under my arm like she was a football and ran around screaming "Touchdown!" Then I plopped her down on their green sofa. "Sorry, Julia. My arms are broken," I said.

"Bow-kin?"

I felt bad lying to a baby. G of L number seven and the Honesty Policy.

"Tired," I said. "Not broken."

"Want food?" Sam asked.

"Of course," I said.

We sat Julia in the middle of the table. Sam gave her a blueberry bagel.

"When you only have six teeth, a bagel lasts a month," he said.

Sam and I ate six crois-sants. We filled three with butter and strawberry jam. The others got ham, mustard, cheddar cheese, pickles, ketchup, jalapeños, cheese sticks, and corn chips.

Julia rolled her bagel off the table and picked up the stick of butter.

"She's eating it like corn on the cob," I said. "Is that okay?"

"She's allowed to have dairy," Sam said.

"But it's the last stick," I said.

"Hand it over, Julia Bear," Sam said. "It's for Mommy's toast."

Julia squeezed. Butter spurted. The top and bot-tom of the stick broke off and fell on her knees. Sam scraped it off with his hand and scraped his hand with a dull butter knife and put it back on the plate.

"Got the Evidence Log, Dog?" I asked.

"Wait here, Amir."

Sam's Chameleon sketches were amazing.

"Good job on the old-lady shoes," I said.

"They're E-Z. I just draw pillow shapes and put shoelaces on them," he said.

"You captured her dumpiness."

"The tall hair picture isn't as good. Flip-flops are harder than they look."

"The butt picture shows her from the back. The FBI can imagine her front," I said.

I looked carefully at the Chameleon's house drawing.

"It's an exact replica of what I remember," Sam said.

"I bet the tower is stuffed with stolen jewels," I said.

"And gold," Sam said.

"And savings bonds," I said. "Plus money and valuable paintings by Vincent van Gogh."

"Can go?" Julia asked.

"Not yet," Sam said.

Julia stood on the table and held her arms out.

"Why did you draw the flowerpots upside down?" I asked.

"Because they WERE upside down," he said.

"A secret signal, no doubt."

Julia reached for my face and asked, "Picnose?"

"Not now," I said.

"Two pots down could mean 'The police are watching us,'" Sam said.

"Four pots up might equal 'The coast is clear,'" I said.

I wrote *Watch out for flowerpots* in the Log.

Sam pointed at the picture. "There's the Chameleon's emergency escape route."

"Tricky," I said. "People probably think it's an ordinary fire escape."

Julia pinched my arm. "Congo?"

"One minute, Julia," Sam said.

I bribed her with a handful of Cinnamon Life from my pocket.

"Got a plan, man?" Sam asked.

"You bet, Robo-Pet," I said. "We're going undercover."

"I vote for mustaches," Sam said.

"No good," I told him. "I had one once. Everybody knew it was me."

"Costumes are in the basement," Sam said.

"For safety, put Baby Julia on top of Laundry Mountain," I said.

She loved it.

"Hats are good disguises," Sam said.

"Skieses," Julia sang.

"Some are. Some aren't," I said. "If we had Mr. and Mrs. Timony's beekeeper hats we'd be set. We could see out. Outsiders couldn't see in. Any good stuff in the utility room?"

"Stay on the mountain," Sam told Julia.

The Alswangs' utility room is a disguise factory. Sam opened the Halloween box.

"Blue robe?" he asked.

"Too wizardy."

"This red suit is small but stretches," he said.

"My mom says red is for people who want attention," I said.

"Usually we do," Sam said. "But not today."

"Waaaaaaaaaaaaa!"

"Julia!" I said.

"We're coming!" Sam yelled.

He tripped over the box. I jumped over him and ran.

Julia was still on the laundry pile. But her body was stuck inside one leg of Mr. Alswang's boxer shorts. Tears were spurting out of her eyeballs. Her nose was running.

Sam flopped down next to her. "It's okay, Julia," he said.

"We're rescuing you," I told her.

I held her by her armpits. Sam yanked the shorts leg off.

Julia bit Sam's arm and said, "Myn bludda." Sometimes she bites out of thankfulness.

She pulled the boxer shorts over her shoes.

"You'll get stuck again, Julia," I said.

"Try on Mom's skirt instead," Sam said.

Julia whipped his arm with a purple sock.

"I'll put the sock on you," Sam said. "Don't weep over it."

That's when I realized. "Mrs. Wilkins told us a top disguise. But I didn't get what she meant until now," I said.

"Explain, Jane," Sam said.

I did.

"Spit on a stick!" Sam said. "What a winner. Also embarrassing."

"Adult agents do it," I said.

"They do what they have to do," Sam said. "It's their job."

"Plus they're loyal to our country," I said.

"And patriotic," Sam said.

"You're automatically patriotic if you're loyal to your country," I said.

"Which we are," Sam said.

"Mrs. Wilkins is a genius," I said.

"E-nusss," Julia said.

"Genius, Julia," Sam said. "She's a genius. You are too."

"Ewe ar poo!" Julia said.

She was pointing at Sam. I laughed until I collapsed on Laundry Mountain.

"You are a funny girl," Sam told Julia.

"Ewe ar poo!" she said.

"If you laugh at what she says, she repeats it," Sam said.

"Good," I said. "*Ewe ar poo* will always be funny."

"Hello down there," Sam's dad yelled. "Has anybody seen the croissants?"

"We did," Sam said.

"Where?" his dad asked.

"In the bread box," Sam told him. "But they're gone now."

When we got upstairs Sam held Julia out.

"Here, Dad. She needs changing."

Julia petted Mr. Alswang's jaw.

He kissed her head and said, "You are my sweet girl."

"Ewe ar poo," Julia said.

"Wasn't that hilarious, Dad? Admit it."

"Hilarious, Sam," Mr. Alswang said.

"Melonhead," Sam said. "Fill our water bottles. I'll get the shoe polish."

"Where are you going?" Mr. Alswang asked.

"To see Mrs. Wilkins," Sam told him.

"Why does Mrs. Wilkins need shoe polish?" Mr. Alswang asked.

"No reason I know," I said.

Julia waved her feet at us.

"Bye, Julia," Sam said.

"Ewe ar poo!" Julia said.

19
UP IN THE ATTIC

"Where's the cake?" Sam asked.

"I left it under the table in your vestibule," I said. "So Julia wouldn't get to it."

Sam opened the Trader Joe's bag. "It's BTG," he said. "Where did you get a cake box?"

"Out of our kitchen trash," I said.

"Looks practically new," he said.

Mrs. Bazoo was at the front desk of the Capitol Hill Retirement Home, on the phone. A lady was ahead of us.

"One of our residents has misplaced her key," Mrs. Bazoo explained to the person on the phone.

"It is not misplaced," the lady said. "The woman with the turban took it."

"Mrs. Solarz," Mrs. Bazoo said, "I am the woman in the turban and I did not take your key."

"Check Mrs. Hennessy," Mrs. Solarz said. "Remember when she stole Mr. Wood's teeth?"

Mrs. Bazoo hung up and said, "Mrs. Solarz, Mr. Peterson is on his way to your apartment to open the door. He will bring you a new key this afternoon."

"It's always interesting over here," I told Mrs. Bazoo.

"Did Mrs. Hennessy really take Mr. Wood's teeth?" Sam asked.

"Mrs. Hennessy likes to collect things," Mrs. Bazoo said. "It's nothing personal."

"We brought your delivery from Baking Divas," I said.

"Perfect," she said. "I was about to call the shop."

"You're going to love it," Sam said.

"I hope so," she said.

We ran out.

"Mistake fixed," I said.

"I'm proud of us," Sam said.

"Ditto," I said. "We took personal responsibility and fixed a problem."

"That shows we have the maturity of fourteen-year-olds," Sam said.

"At least."

Mrs. Wilkins was asleep when we got to her house.

"It's important," I told Molly, extra loud so her mom would wake up.

"You're not at the parade grounds, you know," Mrs. Wilkins yelled.

Molly has a way of looking like she's annoyed.

"Come in, for Pete's sake," Mrs. Wilkins hollered.

I fished around in my Lucky Charms pocket. "I found you an arrowhead."

She looked at both sides.

"Didn't I?"

"No," she said. "It's a pointed rock."

"Sorry," I said.

"I'm not," she said. "I collect pointed rocks."

"How lucky is that?" I said.

"Put it on the hall table next to the picture of me and my incredible flying machine."

It's a propeller plane. Before her hips gave up, Mrs. Wilkins was a pilot.

"Tell me what's happening in the outside world," Mrs. Wilkins said. "I'm stir-crazy."

"Is that worse than regular crazy?" Sam asked.

"It means I'm tired of being stuck inside," she said.

"There's a new pharmacist at Grubb's. His name is Mike," Sam said.

"Is Eddie retiring?" she asked.

"I'll ask him next time," Sam told her.

"Also, Lucy Rose sent a letter," I said. "There is a nosy girl in her cabin so sometimes Lucy Rose fakes

sick and goes to House of Health. She plays cards
with the nurse. Also she got a swimming badge.
Not too interesting."

"Anything is interesting when you're trapped,"
Mrs. Wilkins said. "How's Jonique?"

"Loving math camp," Sam said.

"Plus the Divas got five stars so Jonique gets to
help fold boxes," I said.

"Jonique is a good friend when you're in a jam,"
Mrs. Wilkins said.

"True," I said.

"How did your problem work out?" she asked.

"The cake problem? Perfectly," I said. "We decided they didn't need any cookies."

"You two decided that, did you?" Mrs. Wilkins said.

"They were day-old," I explained.

"Too many sweets are bad for the elderly's health," Sam said. "Also it gives them joy to see us eat."

"So you were doing the old folks a favor by eating their cookies?" Mrs. Wilkins asked.

"That's a good way to put it," I said.

"If you ever start deciding things for me, I'll have you on the next slow boat to China," she said.

"I'll decide everything for you if I get a free boat trip to China," I said. "When do I start?"

"When you're fifty-five," she said.

"But you could be dead by then," I said.

"I expect I will be," she said.

That has to be the medicine talking.

"May I take Sam to the attic?" I said.

"It's one hundred and ten degrees up there," she said.

"Bonus!" Sam told her. "That will break my personal record for heat."

"What's up there that you want?" she asked.

"We're using your idea for Junior Special Agent disguises," I said.

"My idea?"

"Yep. Can we borrow some stuff?" I asked.

"You may borrow anything that I don't like," she said.

"How will we know?" Sam asked.

"Guess you'll have to ask me," she said.

"Can we borrow your binoculars?" I asked.

"If you break them I'll be sorry I said yes," she told us. "And so will you."

"Don't worry," Sam said. "We've had Mrs. Alswang's camera for three entire days. It's still not broken."

"Thank you for the pointed rock," Mrs. Wilkins said.

"Thank you for the help," I told her.

"Can't do much from this chair," she said.

"You've done a lot," I told her.

Sam followed me up the stairs two at a time. I pulled the light string.

"Wow, Cow," Sam said. "We're in Aladdin's cave."

We found almost everything on the rolling

rack. The rest was in a box that said Papua New Guinea.

"Take extra in case some stuff isn't allowed to leave the house."

"Look in that red leather chest," I told Sam. "Get enough for both of us. I'll find shoes."

I threw everything in a plastic bag that said Duty Free.

"Follow me, McGee," I hollered. I jumped from the fourth step to the hall floor. Sam followed so fast he knocked his teeth against my head.

"Shhh!" Molly said. "Mom's asleep."

"We have to wake her up. She wants to check before we borrow."

"Take it," Molly said. "There's nothing worth keeping in that attic."

"You call a stuffed tarantula not worth keeping?" Sam asked.

"Is it in your bag?" Molly said.

"No," I said.

"Then am-scray," she said.

Luckily, I speak Pig Latin.

20
BRAVERY REQUIRED

We went straight to the Conroys' house.

"They're on vacation," I said. "They won't care if we use their backyard for our headquarters. Climb over the fence."

The gate was unlocked but we like to practice.

I dumped the bag out on the picnic table.

"What are you wearing for your disguise?" I asked Sam.

"I'm not wearing anything," he said. "You're the disguise guy. I'm the lookout man."

"The disguise will look more realistic on you," I said.

He socked my arm. Hard.

"No one will know it's you," I said.

"If you're kidnapped by the Chameleon, I'll run for help," he said.

"Rock, paper, scissors," I said. "Loser goes. Winner guards."

"Deal," Sam said.

"E-Z P-Z, nice and breezy," I said.

What I meant was E-Z for me-Z. Sam always picks paper. So I always pick scissors.

For the first time in the history of his life, Sam went for rock.

"Two out of three," I said.

"No chance, Lance," Sam said.

"Promise you'll never tell anyone, even if you're threatened by two hundred dictators."

"Promise," he said.

"No matter what."

"No matter if there are five thousand dictators and they're cannibals and the only way I can save myself is to tell. I still won't," he said. "I would never break the oath of the Junior Special Agent."

"If it's the only way you can save yourself from

being eaten, you can tell," I said. "But that's the only reason."

Sam sat on the Conroys' picnic table. I sat on the bench in front of him.

"Stay still," Sam said. "Unless you want a spotty head."

"Are you almost done?"

"I'm skipping the top to save supplies."

I made him turn around while I changed.

"I feel stupid," I said. "This could be a bad idea."

"You want to check with an adult now?" Sam asked.

"No," I said. "This is a dangling baby."

"There's a dangling baby?" Sam asked.

"One of the times you don't have to ask an adult," I said. "You just save the baby. G for Ls are breakable in emergencies."

"An MW on the loose is a definite emergency," Sam said.

"You can look now," I told him.

He laughed his head off.

"You are a terrible-looking old woman," he said.

That made me feel a little better.

"I never knew earrings hurt," I said.

"How did you make them stick to your ears?" Sam asked.

"Old-lady earrings have jaws," I said. "Once they dig into your flesh, they stay."

"I guess pierced ears weren't invented when Mrs. Wilkins was young," Sam said.

"I need your bungee belt to hold up my dress," I said. "I mean, Mrs. Wilkins's dress that I'm wearing."

"Here," Sam said. "Put the camera and the Evidence Log in your pocketbook."

"Do you think it's okay to take the bows off Mrs. Wilkins's shoes?"

"It would be destruction of private property," Sam said.

Junior Special Agents can never destruct property. Look in the handbook if you don't believe me.

"There's a white shoe-polish streak on your forehead," Sam said.

I spit on my hand and wiped until Sam said it was gone.

"Want me to take a picture so you can see

yourself?" he asked. "Your two-tone head is an automatic laugh."

I put on Mrs. Wilkins's floppy green hat.

"Here's my mom's sunglasses," Sam said.

They are light blue.

"Do I look real?" I asked.

"Let down your shoulders and bend a little," Sam said.

I did.

"Better. But you need two more things." He sat on the picnic table, untied his Chucks, and peeled off his socks.

"I'm not wearing them," I said.

Sam rolled them into balls and threw them at me. Then he pointed at my chest. "You need those things."

"*No* times infinity," I said.

"You won't look believable without them," Sam said.

"Mrs. Wilkins said nobody notices old ladies," I said.

"That's because they look like LADIES."

"Not doing it," I said.

"It's your life that could be kidnapped."

I stuffed the socks under my T-shirt, which was under the leopard-spotted dress.

"Walk elderly style," Sam said.

I made myself stay slow by hardly letting my knees bend.

One hand kept the sunglasses from sliding down my nose sweat. The white gloves blocked a lot of my eyesight. I had to wear them so I wouldn't leave fingerprints. My other hand was holding the pocketbook.

I talked to myself.

"All you have to do is get to the bushes. Act like you're looking at the flowers. No one will suspect. Ladies are known for loving flowers."

I was almost at the figurine museum when I saw the Chameleon.

I wonder if kids can get heart attacks.

I made it to the grass patch, sat down behind the closest bush, and wrote.

10:07 a.m. She's back to being Bethany. Blue skirt. White T-shirt. Huge purse. Red-and-white-striped shoes. Blond wig.

The Chameleon ran up her front steps a lot faster than when she had the big butt. My knees were shaking like Mount Vesuvius. They calmed down after the first hour and fourteen minutes.

Then the door opened.

How many accomplices can one crook have?

I reported this one in the Log.

Curly gray hair. Un-interesting face. Gray

bag. *Dark blue pants, dark blue shirt. Colorful scarf.*
Shape: Round. Age: Between 50 and 80.

Then I saw them.

Red-and-white-striped shoes. Exactly the same.
Proof.

The Chameleon was doing what
I did: The elderly disguise and fake
old-people walk.

I was about to throw up. I made
myself breathe. Due to shaking I
couldn't be still.

11:14 a.m. Chameleon on
the loose.

I bet kids can die from fright. If they're scared
enough. I'm scared enough. I lack bravery.

I opened my pocketbook, took out the camera,
and put it in my lap.

Take a picture. What if she catches me?

She was getting nearer. I pressed the button. Twice.

I got two. She's crooked in one but the side of her face is clear. Not like see-through, like you can see it. The other picture has no head.

Don't look suspicious.

The Chameleon turned left.

11:17 a.m. She's in walking alley. Headed to Eastern Market.

Problem: If I get Sam, I'll lose her. If I don't get Sam, my life could be over.

I have never wanted to not do something as much as I don't want to do this.

If agents only did what they felt like, the FBI wouldn't ever capture anybody. Only I'm sure agents feel like chasing criminals.

Here's what I need: courage.

Then I realized:

My disguise fooled her.

The portable hideouts fooled her.

The FBI is on my side.

When the FBI sees my pictures, the Chameleon's jig will be up.

That gave me confidence. I waved so Sam would know I was following the Chameleon. She was half an alley ahead.

She's stopping. She's turning. She sees me.

I stopped and stared at the ground.

She crossed Seventh Street and went left.

I didn't cross. But I did turn left.

11:20 a.m. Following Chameleon.

I took a picture.

I'm on the case. Professional.

Then I spotted Ashley.

Ashley is the worst girl in my school. She is the worst person in Washington, D.C., to see me wearing a skirt. My stomach shrunk from pain.

Quick. Think.

I flipped around.

Staring at the fence. Not breathing. If she sees me I'm telling my dad we have to move back to Florida.

To keep away from panic I counted by Missis-
sippis.

At ten Mississippi I exhaled. When I got to
twenty-seven, I turned my head two inches.

Ashley was past the alley, nearly to Port City
Java.

*Mrs. Wilkins is right. This old-lady disguise is my
invisibility shield.*

I whipped back around.

No Chameleon.

Do not have a cow.

I ducked behind a privet hedge, ripped off my
disguise, and stuffed it between branches. I kept the
sunglasses on.

Behind me,
someone tapped
my shoulder.

*Please don't be
the Chameleon.*

My heart felt
like it was exploding. I
shifted my eyes toward the tap.

Green jewel bracelet.

"Sheesh! You scared me," I said.

Sam was wearing Mrs. Wilkins's orange suit. The checkered scarf was tied under his chin, hiding his hair.

"You look like my Florida grandma," I said.

"You disappeared!" Sam said. "I thought you were a goner. I jumped into the old-lady clothes and ran to save you."

"I'm sorry I stayed in the onion box when you were being slapped," I said.

"That's okay. Especially since I wasn't," Sam said. "But I should have been a lady and gone with you."

"Then there would have been no one to save me," I said.

"Where's the Chameleon?" Sam asked.

"I lost her," I said. "I bailed when I saw Ashley."

"Ashley's here?" Sam asked. "Can she see me?"

"She's gone," I said. "She didn't know I was me."

"Is the Chameleon in a store?" Sam asked.

"Probably looking for easy ways in and out," I said. "So she can break in and rob in the night."

We made a list in the Log.

Under **NO** I wrote *Dawn Price baby clothes, Monkey's Uncle kids' clothes, Fairy Godmother kids' books & toys. Reason: Chameleon personally told us she is not having a baby.*

Also **NO** for Montmartre restaurant. *Reason: Food comes in too many pieces. Hard getaway. Plus who would steal frog legs? No one.*

Under **MAYBE** I wrote *Rug store. Reason: Rugs roll up for E-Z getaway.*

"I'll go look through the window of the flower store," Sam said.

"Too dangerous," I said.

"I'll hide behind the bush that's shaped like an elephant. Or the donkey bush."

I'd like to know how they grow plants to look like that.

A semi-second later I ran into the street. I grabbed Sam by his orange collar.

"Freeze," I said. "Look across the avenue. By the Metro sign. It's the old lady! That's the Chameleon. Believe me."

"There are too many old ladies in this case," Sam said, which was true. Also funny.

The Chameleon got on the escalator and rode out of sight.

"If only we'd been faster," Sam said.

I felt a little relieved. Also like a wimp. I'm hoping no neighbor calls my mom and says I was grabbing an old person by her neck. Sam went behind the hedge, took off the orange suit and scarf, and shoved them in the bush. "I can't walk around carrying ladies' clothes," he said.

We went to Mrs. Calamaris and asked for a bag.

"Should I cut a hole in the bottom?" she asked.

That was a joke.

On the way home we bought Twizzlers at Grubb's and Twinkies at Jonny and Joon's. Then we speared the Twizzlers through the cream filling.

"When you have a day with this much stress you need a Twink-abob," I told Sam.

To relax my over-beaten heart, we took the long route.

The Deutsch brothers were digging a hole in their yard. Chris yelled, "Looking good, Melonhead."

We practiced hand-walking in the church parking lot. Then the preacher came out. He said we were upsetting the Baptists who were trying to drive.

I dropped Sam at his house.

He walked up the steps backward and said, "See you soon, Loon."

"See you later, Mashed Potater."

I was kicking a rock around the corner when Sam yelled, "Melonhead!"

"What?"

"You forgot to take out my socks."

I could feel my entire head, even my scalp, turning red.

Then I remembered about my brown-and-white hair.

At home, I ran upstairs and locked myself in the

bathroom. When I came out my mom stared at me like I was a talking toaster.

"What?" I said. "Can't a guy take a shower around here without getting eagle-eyed?"

"A guy is welcome to take a shower around here," my mom said. "It's just that this is the first time a guy didn't have to be nagged into it."

21

REPORTING TO THE FBI

This morning Sam and I jumped on the Metro exactly when the doors were starting to close. He was a fraction of an inch from extinction.

"This is exciting," I said.

"I bet we're the first Junior Special Agents to discover an MW," Sam said.

We went through FBI security to Officer Yang's desk.

"Junior Special Agent Adam Melon and Junior Special Agent Samuel Alswang reporting," I said.

We showed our badges.

Officer Yang smiled.

"We have a confidential report for Agent Atkin," Sam said.

"I see that," Officer Yang said. "It says on the package."

That was my idea.

"Agent Atkin is in with the big bosses," Officer Yang told us.

"Perfect. The bosses will want to see this evidence," I said.

"No doubt," Officer Yang said. "But I'm under Do Not Disturb orders."

"Oh, we don't mind waiting," Sam said.

"They'll be at it a long while," Officer Yang said.

"Once they read our report they'll put out a dragnet, right?" I asked.

"I can't say," Officer Yang told us. "I haven't read the report."

Sam and I had a supersonic brain exchange.

"You have our permission," I said.

Evidence collected by Junior Special Agent Adam Melon, aka Melonhead, and Junior Special Agent Samuel K. Alswang

Most Wanted FFJ: The Chameleon
Hideout: 748 Eighth Street, S.E.
Identifying marks: Could not see mole.
Height: Middle-size. (Couldn't measure.)
Weight: Ditto. (Couldn't weigh.)

Disguises:
1. Shorts or skirt. Yellow wig. (Alias: Bethany Lewis.) (Metro.)
2. Tan shirt. Mouse-colored hair. Black skirt. Old-lady shoes. Shape: Skinny. (Eighth Street S.E.)

3. Fattening black pants. High heels (carrying). Flip-flops (wearing). Tall red hair. (Eighth Street S.E.)
4. Orange shorts. Blue shirt. (In her yard.) Blond wig (Bethany Lewis style).
5. Blond wig (again). Blue skirt. White shirt. Striped red-and-white shoes. (Flat.) (Crossing street near house.)
6. Gray Hair. Black pants. Striped flat shoes (again).

Next caper: Probably Figurine Museum.
Accomplice: Man. Unknown.
Height: Between 5′ and 8 or so inches and 6′ 2″.
Weight: Not fat. Not skinny.
Clothes: Plaid shorts, red sneakers.
Voice: Sneaky.
Remarks: Overly interested in figurines.

"Well-done sketch of the house," Officer Yang said. "Interesting photo of the alleged Chameleon's alleged backside."

"Sam did the drawings," I said.

"The alleged accomplice has tough-looking sideburns," Officer Yang said.

"Do you know a lot about alleged crooks?" I asked.

"I know a fair amount about real crooks," he said.

"How come they go for the life of crime instead of the life of regular people?" I asked.

"Personally, I think it depends on the crook," Officer Yang said. "Some are bad apples; some start small for kicks and one day they need money and graduate to stealing cars. Others like planning and getting away with it. There are even those who tell themselves a big business won't miss a few million dollars. So why not?"

"Which type is the Chameleon?" Sam asked.

"They'll find out when they catch her," Officer Yang said.

"Today's the day for that," I said. "Once Agent Atkin reads the report, how long will it take to arrest her into custody? The Chameleon, I mean. Not Agent Atkin."

"I don't expect an arrest anytime soon," Officer Yang said.

"But it's all in the file," Sam said.

Officer Yang shut the folder. "What you have here is a fine start, but it's light on evidence," he said.

"You call that light?" I asked.

"The FBI is grateful for your help," he said. "But leave the Chameleon to the senior agents. Go enjoy what's left of your summer."

"You'll give Agent Atkin the folder?" I asked.

"The minute I see her," he said.

Sam and I walked to Chinatown. We sat on a doorstep and split a pork bun.

"What other evidence could they need?" Sam asked.

"Fingerprints," I said. "Maybe a front-side photo."

"How can we get them?" Sam asked.

"The first thing we need are secret identities that aren't cardboard boxes or skirts," I said.

22
MADE OF MONEY

I had a nightmare last night. I bet that happens to all agents when they're closing in on an FFJ.

Then I couldn't sleep. My mind was crowded. I went over things in my head.

"Morning, Sport," my dad said. "Have a donut."

I picked chocolate cream.

My dad watched me load my pockets with Lucky Charms.

"Any big plans for today?" he asked.

"I'm going to the bank and to the Divas," I said.

Sam met me at Jimmy T's.

"I could go for a Dum Dum," he said. "But there's

no time to go to the bank. I figured out a way to get the Chameleon's fingerprints."

"Come on. It's a quick walk to the bank," I said.

"If I go, I get the sucker," Sam said. "How much money are you putting in?"

"I'm getting it out."

"How much?"

"All of it," I said.

"Did you catapult a baseball through Mrs. Lee's window again?" Sam asked.

"Nope," I said.

"They don't give out lollipops when you un-deposit money," Sam said.

"I know," I said.

"You must be buying something important," he said. "Is it a listening device?"

I told him. He tried to talk me out of it.

We were in line at the bank when Sam said, "I'll pay half."

When Mr. Franklin looked at our withdrawing slips, all he said was "How do you want it?"

What does that mean?

"How do we want it?" Sam said.

"A ten and two twenties?" Mr. Franklin asked.

"We want it in one-dollar bills," I said.

Mr. Franklin counted out loud. Every time he got to ten he made a little pile. Then he divided the cash and put it in two envelopes.

"There's twenty-five dollars and thirty-three cents in each one," he said.

"Thank you," I said.

Sam took one dollar out of his envelope. "I want this in a dollar coin," he said.

"Same for me," I said.

Mr. Franklin took our money and handed us two coins.

"If I can't be an inventor for the FBI I'm going to be a bank teller," I told Mr. Franklin.

"You must like math," he said.

"No," I told him. "I like money."

Sam pulled two Now Serving numbers at the Baking Divas.

"One for me. One for Melonhead," he told Aunt Frankie.

"I appreciate that," she said.

We picked all our favorites.

"Two Key Lime cookies, two Sassy Molassies, and two Co-Co-Nutty-Buddies," I said.

"Two Snowscones," Sam said. "Two Monumentals and two Why Nuts?"

"Two Sweetie Pies, two Sweet Joniques, two Tripple-Dipple-Dos," I said.

"You're getting a middle-size box?" Aunt Frankie asked.

"Large," I said. "Two Smart Blondies, one piece of Lola's Lively Lemon Cake, two Coffee Toffee Bars, please."

"Two Nutella Knots," Sam said. "Two PBJs and two Greek Weddings."

"And one Blue Moon," I said.

It cost so much I felt like my brain was floating.

"We still have our dollar coins," Sam said.

"Is Jonique here?" I asked.

"Vacation Bible School started this morning," Aunt Frankie said. "But it's only a half day. She'll be here for lunch."

Mrs. McBee walked up to the counter. "I need

to talk to you two," she said. "Come to the back room."

It was the first time I didn't want to talk to her.

She unlocked the Employees Only door.

She pointed at two red plastic milk crates.

"Sit," she said.

She sat behind her desk.

"Mrs. Bazoo called this morning," she said.

My stomach felt like it was sliding into my lap.

Mrs. Wilkins said her cake smelled like Paris. But she didn't taste it.

"What did she say?" Sam asked.

He has a load of courage.

"She said the Three Kings Cake was good," Mrs. McBee said. "Called it luscious."

Relief.

Sam was fidgeting with the string tied around our cookie box.

"She said it was better

than the Three Kings Cake she had on her honeymoon."

"Really?" I asked.

"She thought she tasted cloves," Mrs. McBee said.

"Is that bad?" I asked.

"Not at all," Mrs. McBee said. "Mrs. Bazoo grew up in Indonesia. She helped her mom harvest and grind clove buds."

"Clove buds?" Sam said.

"Cloves look like flowers when they're on the tree," she said.

"Garlic grows on trees?" I said.

"Cloves grow on trees. Garlic grows in the ground," Mrs. McBee said. "But to get back to Mrs. Bazoo's call. She said the oddest thing."

"What?" Sam asked.

"She said, 'We were trying to decide what the marzipan decorations were supposed to be.' I said, 'Roses. What did you think they were?' And she said, 'Snakes. Curled-up snakes.'"

"Snakes?" I said.

I wanted to say they looked like roses. But that would be admitting we made them.

"Red snakes with green legs."

"What did you say?" I asked.

"I offered to give her money back," Mrs. McBee said.

"Did she take it?" Sam asked.

"No. She ordered a cake for her mother's birthday in September. Wants it to be exactly the same. Except no snakes."

"That's great," I said.

"Trouble is, I don't know how to make that cake," she said.

"Sure you do," Sam said. "You made it before."

"No. I don't," Mrs. McBee said.

"But our cake was the same as yours," I blurted.

"What happened to my cake?"

"It got eaten," I said.

"But first it fell out of a tree," Sam said.

"It was an accident," I said. "An unavoidable accident."

"Accidents do happen," Mrs. McBee said. "But

they are considerably more likely to happen to cakes put in trees."

"Like my dad says, the good news is that we learned from this incident," I said.

"What do you know now that you didn't know before?" Mrs. McBee asked.

"Number one: how easy it is for a cake to fall out of a tree," I said.

"Number two: we learned to cook a cake," Sam said.

"That Mrs. Bazoo loved," I said, to remind her of the praise.

"That was your fine luck," Mrs. McBee said. "If Mrs. Bazoo hadn't, she would have blamed Baking Divas. And if J. A. Fischer had ordered that cake, I expect he would have been more judgmental. There is a big difference between four stars and five stars."

"We should have told you right off the bat," I said.

"We shouldn't have been scared of you," Sam said.

"Oh, there was good reason to be scared of me," Mrs. McBee said. "When I found out, I was hopping mad. And you don't want to hear what my sister said. But you should have told me anyway."

"Next time we will," I said. "Not that we're having a next time."

"Remember it. This will happen again and you're going to have to decide what to do."

"It can't happen again," I said, "because we will never put a cake in a tree again."

"You will make more mistakes in your life," she said. "Probably many."

"I predict that's true," I said. "Are we fired?"

"I have to think about this," Mrs. McBee said.

"We're sorry," I said. "Very, very sorry."

"Sorry times infinity," Sam said.

"Now tell me what you put in your Three Kings Cake."

"Flour, butter, and cinnamon," Sam said.

"Clove powder, allspice, baking soda, and baking powder," I said.

"We traded the sugar for honey, like you did,"

Sam said. "But we ran out. We skipped the last half cup."

"That's fine. Honey is sweeter than sugar," Mrs. McBee said. "But so far your cake is my cake."

Then I remembered.

"Plus a can of tomato soup," I said. "But that was a mistake."

"Tomato soup?" Mrs. McBee asked.

"The soup was supposed to be Pop's snack," Sam said. "But it was on the counter with the ingredients."

"What a revolting combination," she said. "You didn't ask yourselves why would we put soup in a cake?"

"No," Sam said, "we didn't."

"I'll make one and see what Mrs. Bazoo thinks. If she likes it and I love it, I'll put it on the menu."

"You should call it Accidental Cake," I said.

"I'm thinking about Tree Kings Cake."

I high-fived Sam. "We'll be famous," Sam said.

"There's one more thing to explain," I said. "We ate the cookies without knowing we did."

"You didn't know you were eating the cookies?" Mrs. McBee said.

"We didn't know we were eating ALL the cookies," I said.

"Except for four. We gave those to Mrs. Wilkins," Sam said. "And she IS retired."

"And one was taken by a squirrel," I said.

"You ate after a squirrel?" Mrs. McBee said. "Oh, I did not need to know that."

"I had to tell you," I said. "It's a G for L. Honesty Is the Only Policy."

"Good for Gs and Ls," Mrs. McBee said. "Whatever they are. And don't worry about the cookies. They were day-olds."

"Don't worry?" Sam said.

"I shouldn't send so many sweets over there anyway. Too much sugar isn't good for anyone."

You know about *stunned silence*? I had it.

"You mean we can eat all the day-olds?" Sam said. "Hot diggity dog on a log."

"I don't mean any such thing," Mrs. McBee said.

"But we just bought replacements," I said.

I thought she was going to say, "Have a refund."

But what she said was "That was an expensive lesson."

"That's okay," I said. "I already have ten ideas about how to remake our savings."

"Let's glide, Clyde," Sam said.

We sat on the Divas' patio and ate the ten biggest cookies. Then we retied the box. I balanced it on top of my helmet.

"Hold on to the sides for safety," Sam said.

We skateboarded downhill, through the automatic doors, and across the Retirement Home carpet. We stopped when Sam's board plowed the front desk.

"Special delivery, Mrs. Bazoo," I said.

On the way out Sam said, "I think Mrs. McBee's going to feel bad when she finds out we had to put the cake in the tree due to being on a stakeout of an MWFFJ."

"That's true, McGoo," I said.

23

A LITTLE HELP FROM A FRIEND

I smacked my own forehead.

"Mrs. Wilkins was giving us another message," I said.

"When?" Sam asked.

"When she was going on about the greatness of Lucy-Rose-and-Jonique," I said.

"I get tired of that conversation," Sam said.

"Mrs. Wilkins was hinting that we should let Jonique help us," I told him.

"Why?"

"Because the Chameleon has no idea who Jonique is," I said. "Plus Jonique's a thinker. She fits in small places and screams so loud she gives people headaches."

"That will be handy if she gets captured," Sam said. "But she is untrained by the FBI."

"True," I said. "But she's loyal and that's a quality."

I could not believe Jonique was hard to convince.

"It's an honor that we are asking you," Sam told her.

"I'm scared of criminals," she said.

"Capitol Hill is in danger," I said.

"Capitol Hill our neighborhood, or Capitol Hill the government?" she asked.

"Both," Sam said.

"You are one hundred percent POSITIVE the Chameleon is a criminal?" Jonique asked.

"One hundred percent times infinity," I said.

"She wouldn't wear disguises if she wasn't a crook," Sam said.

"It's called going incognito," Jonique said.

"Well, FBI agents go incognito," I said. "But the Chameleon is no agent. Believe me."

"She told us she spies on the neighborhood," Sam said. "And she's probably going to rob the figurine museum."

"I've never heard of the figurine museum," Jonique said.

"There's a load of museums in Washington," I said.

"She will not stop with figurines," Sam said.

"She could be plotting to swipe the U.S. Constitution out of the U.S. Archives," I said. "Or the *Wizard of Oz* ruby shoes out of the Smithsonian."

"We personally heard her talk about the Hope Diamond," Sam said.

"Why can't the FBI get her?" Jonique said.

"They'll do the actual arresting," I said. "We're the evidence men."

"They let Junior Agents be in charge of proof?" Jonique said. "I think that's nuts."

"Junior SPECIAL Agents," I said.

"You'll be safe as safe," Sam said. "We'll be watching you through Mrs. Wilkins's binoculars."

"All right, already," Jonique said.

"All you have to do is watch her house. If anybody comes out, take their picture with Sam's mom's camera," I said. "Make sure you get her face. From the front."

"Once I get the picture, I'm done," she said. "Do not expect me to be getting fingerprints."

"That's the easy part," I said.

Sam explained.

"It's a crackpot idea," Jonique said. "Just because Scotch tape is clear doesn't mean it's unnoticeable. If somebody wrapped my railing in double-sided tape, it would be the first thing I saw."

"Just follow the Chameleon," I said.

"If she gets near me, I'm running like a cheetah," Jonique said.

"You're going to be a hero," I told her.

"I don't want to be a hero," she said. "I want to be a math teacher."

Our spy station was inside Eastern Market, next

to the cheese man, behind a door. Luckily the door has a window.

"We trade turns every five minutes," I said.

"The person not watching does the Log," Sam said.

By 1:45 we had written *Nothing Is Happening* nineteen times.

"It would be easier to observe if customers didn't keep coming and going," Sam said.

"Heads up!" I said. "Jonique is coming through the alley. A lady is behind her."

I turned the focusing wheel. "It's the Chameleon," I said. "In her Bethany disguise."

Jonique ran like she had motorized legs.

The Chameleon's in front of Baking Divas. Accomplice is by the flower box! They're going inside.

Jonique flew through the market door. She was scared.

"We're sorry, Jonique," I said. "We shouldn't have asked you to do it. You're not a trained agent."

"You don't have to trail her anymore," Sam said.

"You can't dump me now," Jonique said.

"She's not alone," Sam said. "The accomplice is with her."

"I saw him," Jonique said.

"Are you sure you have enough courage to do this?" I asked.

She nodded. "I'm not doing it for you guys," she said. "I'm doing it for my country."

"Here's the Log and a mini-pencil," I said. "And don't worry. I'll guard the front of the bakery."

"I'll be in the alley, watching the patio in case they make a break for it," Sam said.

24

A BREAK IN THE CASE

Jonique was in the bakery for seventeen minutes. When she came out she was carrying a white box. The Evidence Log was on top. Her legs looked shaky.

I toucanned.

"Did they catch you?" I asked.

"Keep walking," she said. "Don't stop until we get to Capitol Hill Antiques."

Sam caught up with us.

We sat on the curb.

"It's okay if you lost your nerve, Jonique," I said.

"I kept my nerve," she said. "And I am an awesome force."

"That's not what I expected," Sam said.

"Me either," she told us. "Read the Log."

Chameleon ordered a full-size Sweetie Pie, BTG.

C said visitors are coming. A got 2 coffees, 2 Blueberry Blisses. EI.

"That stands for eat-in," Jonique said. "C and A are short for Chameleon and Accomplice."

C & A on patio. Sitting at red umbrella table.

I backed up my chair for better hearing. C looked at me like I was an eavesdropper. I moved back, watched her reflection in my spoon, like Melonhead said. Can't see anything except upside-down heads.

"You couldn't hear?" I asked.

"I heard some," Jonique said. "Keep reading."

C: It's too risky.

A: I've done riskier jobs.

C: One slipup and we end up swimming in our own blood.

A: Don't be so negative.

Couldn't hear anything until C & A were leaving.
C: I'm getting Handy Harry to do it.
P.S. C's hair covers her neck so I don't know about
any tattoo.

"Holy moly, Jonique! This is major evidence!" I said.

"Great job," Sam said.

"I know," Jonique said.

I pointed at the box. "Are those cookies?"

"Nope," she said.

Sam opened the lid. "Baking Divas mugs?"

"Don't touch!" Jonique said. "They're covered with fingerprints. The Chameleon's cup is the one with lipstick on it."

"How did you pick them up?" I asked.

"I put a fork through the handle," she said. "I'm not a Junior Agent, but I know some things."

I started to say "Junior SPECIAL Agent" for the fiftieth time but I didn't.

"We're sharing the reward with you," I said. "Even Steven."

"I should say so," Jonique said. "And make sure the FBI gives back the mugs. My mom says they cost a pretty penny."

"That's cheap," I said.

"I know," Jonique said. "But she doesn't like buying new ones."

"People won't believe kids caught the Chameleon," I said.

"I wonder if they have TVs at Lucy Rose's camp?" Jonique said. "Because if they do, and she sees us, she'll fall out of her sneakers."

"It's too late for the FBI today," I said. "But tomorrow, when we turn in the evidence, people will be safe in this town."

"Thanks to us," Sam said. "And Jonique."

"We'll meet at the Divas in the morning," I said.

"I have Vacation Bible School," Jonique said. "Come at twelve-thirty."

25

PICKING UP OUR REWARD

We got to Baking Divas early.

"Don't you boys look handsome," Mrs. McBee said.

"They're getting mature, Mama," Jonique said.

"I got this blazer for my cousin's bar mitzvah," Sam said. "The sleeves came down to my wrists in May."

"I like it when shirt cuffs show," Jonique said.

She was wearing a yellow dress with green flowers, and sandals. For Jonique, that is dressing as usual. "I put the mug evidence in this Divas bag," she said.

"Think you boys can handle a delivery?" Mrs. McBee asked.

"We cannot say no," I whispered.

"It's going to your house, Sam," Mrs. McBee said. "I thought we'd start small."

"E-Z P-Z, Aunt Louisie," I said.

We ran.

"Melonhead, throw your jacket under the porch," Sam said. "Or my parents will wonder."

Sam's dad gave us one dollar for a tip. I took it because I have the safest pocket.

Jonique patted Julia on the head and said, "You're cute."

"Ewe ar poo!" Julia said.

"Ewe are hilarious," I told her.

"See you later, baby alligator," Sam said.

"Why did your sister call me poo?" Jonique asked.

"She's in a phase," Sam said.

We talked on the walk to the Metro.

"I'm glad I'm done following that Chameleon. She scares me to bits," Jonique said.

"I bet the FBI director makes a speech about us being American heroes," Sam said.

"Do we get the reward as soon as we tell them?" Jonique asked.

"Probably," I said.

"I hope they give us a giant check like they have on the telethon," Jonique said.

"I always wanted one of those," I said.

When we got to Union Station, Jonique said, "I always wish this was my house. My room would be on that balcony."

"You'd have statues in your room?" Sam asked.

"Wouldn't you?" she asked.

"No," I said.

"The air-conditioning feels good on my sweat," Sam said.

"No doubt, but if I'm going to be meeting directors, I need to re-fresh myself," Jonique said.

I do not understand the ways of girls.

"Don't dawdle," Sam said. "While she's in there, let's collect pamphlets at the Travelers Aid booth."

"I have all of them," I said. "You go. I'll check if All-American Cuisine has a mint bowl."

My mom says eating at All-American Cuisine would be a waste. It only got two and a half stars.

The welcome lady was not at her stand but the mints were. I took two handfuls. You can help yourself. They're free. I put two in my mouth and the rest in my pocket.

I was doing arm exercises on the railing between regular people and people waiting for tables. My reflection in All-American Cuisine's window made me look like my shoulders were two feet wide. The reflecting balcony soldiers looked like my guards. They're holding shields in front of themselves. I think they're nudists underneath.

That was when I choked. I could see my reflection gagging. No noise came out of my mouth. I couldn't get my breath. Suddenly I was grabbed from the back and punched between my ribs.

Blue candy flew out of my mouth.

"You are okay?" the waiter said.

"Yes," I said.

He ran to pick a wet mint out of a lady's hair.

I heard a mom telling her kids that I was proof of what happens to people who fool around with food in their mouth.

But the choking was not due to mints. The cause was on the other side of the window, at a table, wearing a yellow wig with a wrapped-around braid on top. It looked like a little hair hat. She had a purple cloth covering her shoulders. No doubt about the necklace. It was the famous Black Diamond of Donegal.

The accomplice was sitting next to her. *They're going to catch a train and escape this town forever.*

Do something.

Supersonic brain-to-brain emergency messages:

1. *Sam, come back!*
2. *Jonique, hurry up!*
3. *Chameleon: Slow down!*

They were sharing a brownie with ice cream.

Union Station is always crowded with police. Now I can't see one.

The Chameleon put down her fork. The accomplice ate the rest. The waiter brought them a black folder.

Once they pay, they'll leave. Once they leave, it's goodbye MWFFJ.

What are my choices?

If I leave to find Sam, they'll escape. The ladies' bathroom is closer but I can't go in. Where is the FBI when you need them?

Then I remembered. *I am the FBI.*

I tore a page out of the Log and used my mini-golf pencil to write.

Dear Sam and Jonique,
    MWFFJ is at All-American. I'm going in.
Don't worry. She can't kidnap me in front of a

whole restaurant. DO NOT COME IN. *You are the guards.*

I folded the note in quarters and took it to the welcome lady.

"If a kid named Sam or a girl named Jonique comes here, will you give them this note?" I said.

"Are your parents in the restaurant?" she asked.

I nodded. "They're waiting for me."

I had to say that. Because what if she said I had to leave?

I got the dollar Sam's dad gave us. "For your tip," I told the lady.

Onetwothreego!

I sucked in all the air I could hold and walked my spaghetti legs through the door.

Remember the Code of the Melons.

The waiter was picking up the folder. "I'll be right back with your credit card, Mrs. Mangini."

Now she's stealing credit cards!

My feet felt heavy. I stared at the carpet dots and wished for nerve.

Halfway to the table.

My stomach's flapping.

Ignore it.

I stopped smack in front of the table. Then I pointed dead at her. I started to talk. Only a squawk came out. I swallowed my spit.

"I know who you are!" I said. "And I know what you're up to!"

Her eyes popped.

"Melonhead?" she said.

I was wrong about her not kidnapping me in front of people. The Chameleon grabbed my hand and leaned in. Her nose was one inch from mine. Her smile was as fake as her hair.

"Do not speak," she hissed. "Not one word."

Say something.

I squeaked.

She stood up. "We are leaving quietly," she said. "Do not make a scene."

She walked quickly with me in tow. I bet it looked friendly.

Yell. Sit down. Refuse to move. Scream.

I knew what to do. But I kept walking.

We passed the welcome lady.

"I see you found your mom," she said.

She is not my mother!

"He's a great kid," the welcome lady said. "And a good tipper."

The Chameleon smiled and kept steering me as she moved along.

"People know where I am," I told her.

"Quiet."

Most people were rushing from the front to the back where the trains are. We were cutting across the huge lobby. Somebody's suitcase wheel ran over my sneaker. That made me think of my dad pulling his three-and-a-half-wheel suitcase. I purposely stubbed my sneakers on the marble. We passed Travelers Aid. No Sam.

Jonique's probably still in the bathroom.

We went by the bookstore.

Why did I think Sam would get that note? Jonique doesn't even know I was at All-American.

The Chameleon aimed me at the farthest corner and stopped in front of a restaurant called Jack's Good Eats.

For a second I had hope. Then I saw the sign under the Jack's Good Eats sign. It said COMING SOON!

Not soon enough to save me.

"Sit on the edge of that planter," she said.

Sit. Make a plan. Run.

The Chameleon stood over me like an evil vulture.

"You were going to expose me!" she said. "In front of everyone."

"You won't get away with this," I said.

"I've been getting away with it for ten years," she said. "And you are not going to destroy everything I have worked for!"

"What are you going to do with me?" I asked.

She ignored that.

"How did you figure out who I am?" she asked.

"We've been following you," I said. "Your disguises didn't fool us."

"Who's us?" she asked.

"My partner," I said. "And don't ask who he is. I won't betray him."

"Sam," she said. "The kid I met on the subway. Did you tell anyone else?"

"The FBI," I said. "A top agent took our report."

Her forehead wrinkled.

"I'm not worried about the FBI," she said.

"I'm sure everybody on the Most Wanted List says that," I told her.

"What list?"

"You are nothing but a Fugitive from Justice!" I said.

The Chameleon flung her head back and laughed like the maniac she is.

She's demented!

"I'm on the FBI's Most Wanted List?"

"You didn't know?" I said. "Your picture is where everybody can see it. You'll be apprehended in no time."

"Apprehended?" she said.

"It means captured," I told her.

"I know that," she said.

This is a good time to do the citizen's arrest.

"You are a nervy kid," she said.

"I am not fooled by your charm," I said.

The Chameleon put her hands on my shoulders and said, "Junior Agent."

"Junior Special Agent," I said.

"Junior Special Agent," she said. "I will reveal my secret identity. But first you must promise."

"Your identity is no secret," I said. "And I don't make deals with crooks."

Then I realized something. *I am brave.*

"This is for your ears only, Special Agent," the Chameleon said.

I gave her the look of dry ice. "FBI agents work with partners. Telling me is the same as telling Sam."

She told me anyway. It made my brain spin.

That's when I heard the screech of sneakers on marble.

"Great work!" Sam shouted. "You captured her!"

"Sort of," I said.

"Shouldn't we tie her up or something?" Sam asked.

"Sam," I said.

"We can use my shoelaces," he said.

"Sam," I said again.

"What?"

"Meet J. A. Fischer."

"J. A. Fischer is a man," Sam said. "Everybody knows that."

"She goes by a lot of names," I said.

26
THE SHOCKING TRUTH

"I don't get it," Sam said.

"I am forced to trust you with my secret," the Chameleon whispered.

Sam pointed to the Evidence Log. "Get ready to write, Melonhead."

"You have to take the Oath of Silence," the Chameleon said.

"You should take it," I said to Sam. "Believe me."

"An oath is a serious thing," Sam said.

"Yes, it is," Ms. Lewis said. "I know I can count on Junior Special Agents to keep it."

"Unless someone is in danger," Sam said.

"Of course," she said.

"If you're a crook, I'm in danger," he said. "So I could tell."

"Just take the oath," I said.

Two minutes later, Sam was in triple shock.

"You get paid to criticize food?" he asked.

"It's a volunteer job," I explained. "The food is the pay."

"Actually, I get paid in money," she said.

"You're kidding," Sam said.

"How much?" I asked.

"I'm not kidding and I'm not saying," she said.

"Is it more than ten thousand bucks?" I asked.

"What's your real name?" Sam asked.

"Bethany Lewis. J. A. Fischer is my pen name. I make restaurant reservations under many different names."

"You should make one for Mr. I. P. Daily," I said. "That would be hilarious."

"A laugh riot," she said.

"You wear disguises," Sam said.

"I have to," she said. "If restaurant owners recognized me I'd get special treatment."

"I would tell them if I were you," I said.

"My job is to get the same attention and the same food everybody else gets."

"If you don't want attention, be an old lady," I said.

"Can you order anything you want?" Sam asked. "Like ten pies?"

"I order one of everything," she said.

"At once?" I asked.

"No. I go to every restaurant several times."

"You know," I told her, "that could be why your stomach puffs out."

Her eyebrows moved up.

"I am not fooled by charm, either," she said.

"You don't have to eat things you despise, right?" Sam asked.

"I try it all," she said. "The good, the bad, and the horrible."

"You should bring people with bad taste," I told her. "They could be like portable garbage disposals."

"I once ate stewed alligator," she said. "Another time I ate snake."

"Raw?" I said.

"No," she said.

"Did the snake look like a snake?" I asked.

"Exactly," she said. "Coiled on the plate."

"I'd eat a snake," I said.

"Not the whole thing," Sam said. "And not ones that are pets."

"Not the rattle," I said. "Or the head. I'd eat the middle. Maybe."

"What did it taste like?" Sam asked.

"Not like chicken," Ms. Lewis said.

"I wouldn't think so," I told her.

"Why do you tell people to eat frog legs?" Sam asked.

"Sometimes I tell them not to eat them," she said. "Depends on the chef."

Then she looked at Sam. "Do we have a deal?"

"Yes," he said.

"I'm sorry I almost revealed your incognito, Ms. Lewis," I said.

"You were doing your duty," she said. "There's no reason to be embarrassed."

"Why would we be embarrassed?" Sam asked.

"You have to admit, the evidence was against you," I said.

"It takes courage to confront a criminal," she said.

"And courage to confront a food critic who looks like a criminal," Sam said.

"But don't do either one ever again," she said. "Leave crooks to the police. Leave food critics alone."

"All the time or just when they're in a restaurant?" I asked.

"Crooks? All the time. Food critics, when they're anywhere that serves food," she said.

We heard yelling.

"Melonhead!"

"Jonique!" I waved.

"The accomplice is following me!" she yelled.

Ms. Lewis looked across the station. "That accomplice is my husband," she said. "I call him Andrew. You may call him Mr. Revera."

When Jonique realized the lady next to me was the Chameleon in disguise, she stopped short. "They've got us surrounded," she said.

When you are not allowed to say something, that is the only thing in your mind.

"Don't panic, Jonique," Sam said. "She's our friend."

"You made friends with an MW?" Jonique squealed. "Are you nuts?"

"It was a case of mistaking identity," I told her.

Jonique pointed at Ms. Lewis. "You're not a Fugitive from Justice?" she asked.

"No," Ms. Lewis said. "I'm not."

"Then who is Handy Harry?" Jonique said. She had that accusing tone. Her fists were on her hips. I could tell she was dead scared.

"Handy Harry?" Mr. Revera said.

"YOU'RE Handy Harry?" Jonique said. Her eyes looked wild.

"No," Mr. Revera said. "He's coming to paint our shutters next week. My wife is afraid of heights and thinks I should be too."

"One slip of your foot and it's blood and gore," she said.

Jonique looked at me like I was slug pie.

"It was an honest mistake," I said.

"It could happen to anybody," Sam said.

"My mistake was listening to boys," Jonique said.

"I am so embarrassed I wish I could crawl in a bag and hide until I'm twenty-two years old."

"I am not following this conversation," Mr. Revera said.

"I'll explain it on the walk home," Ms. Lewis said.

"We don't mind walking with you," I said. "My house is on the way."

When you leave out the J. A. Fischer part of the story, Sam and I sound like Superagents. We couldn't leave it in due to Jonique being with us. Sort of with us. She was walking ahead with Ms. Lewis and Mr. Revera. I could hear her apologizing for knowing us.

"Do you think she's mad at us?" Sam asked.

"Yes," I said. "But she shouldn't be. Probably every agent would make the same mistake."

"Can you believe we got to meet J. A. Fischer?" Sam said.

"My mom would go berserk with joy if I told her," I said. "But I'm a Man of my Word. That's in the Code of the Melons."

"The Alswangs don't have a code," Sam said.

"But Junior Special Agents are not oath busters. Ten thousand cannibal dictators could not get me to reveal my knowledge."

I was giving Sam a ride on top of the Keenans' recycling trash can when Ms. Lewis stopped and pointed across the street and said, "Do you know that lady?"

"Mom alert," Sam said. "Did we do something?"

"How should I know?" I said.

"Who is DB?" Mr. Revera asked.

"Don't worry, Mom," I yelled. "My jacket's fine. I still have one of the gold buttons."

Jonique curled her hands around her mouth and yelled, "Mrs. Melon! Meet Ms. Lewis and Mr. Revera." Then she told Ms. Lewis, "That's Melon-head's mom."

Adults can talk about her manners for decades. Jonique's. Not my mom's. Adults don't talk about each other's manners, even when they're bad.

"Green light," Jonique said. We crossed.

"Nice to meet you," Ms. Lewis said.

Mr. Revera pointed at me and said, "He's a wild man."

"Not anymore," my mom said. "Adam and Sam have had excellent judgment ever since my husband came up with the Guidelines for Life."

"Really?" Ms. Lewis said.

"Before the Guidelines it was one goofy idea after another," my mom said.

"And after?" Mr. Revera asked.

"It was still one goofy idea after another, but now they think before they act."

Mr. Revera and Ms. Lewis laughed.

"Mrs. Melon," Sam said. "Don't you think this calls for ice cream cones?"

"Can we go to Serendoubledipity?" I asked.

She nodded.

"Ms. Lewis," Sam said. "You and Mr. Revera should come with us."

"They have seventeen flavors," Jonique said. "You'll love it like anything."

"Believe her," Sam said.

I looked Ms. Lewis in the eyes.

"If you don't believe her, ask J. A. Fischer," I said. "*He* gave it four and a half stars."

ABOUT THE AUTHOR

Katy Kelly has never been a Junior Special Agent for the FBI, but as a teenager she worked, briefly and unsuccessfully, as a store detective. Katy lives in Washington, D.C., with her artist husband and their two daughters. This is her seventh book for young readers and the third in the Melonhead series.

ABOUT THE ILLUSTRATOR

Gillian Johnson has never been to FBI headquarters in Washington, D.C., but she hopes to make the trip one day. Gillian lives in Oxford, England, with her husband and their two sons.

Don't miss the next book in the Melonhead series!

Available now from Delacorte Press!